Ann Cleeves

Ann Cleeves is the author behind ITV's VERA and BBC One's SHETLAND. She has written over twenty-five novels, and is the creator of detectives Vera Stanhope and Jimmy Perez – characters loved both on screen and in print. Her books have now sold over one million copies worldwide.

Ann worked as a probation officer, bird observatory cook and auxiliary coastguard before she started writing. She is a member of 'Murder Squad', working with other British northern writers to promote crime fiction. In 2006 Ann was awarded the Duncan Lawrie Dagger (CWA Gold Dagger) for Best Crime Novel, for *Raven Black*, the first book in her Shetland series. In 2012 she was inducted into the CWA Crime Thriller Awards Hall of Fame. Ann lives in North Tyneside.

Ann Cleeves

MURDER IN
PARADISE

BELL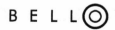

First published in 1988 by Century

This edition published 2014 by Bello
an imprint of Pan Macmillan, a division of Macmillan Publishers Limited
Pan Macmillan, 20 New Wharf Road, London N1 9RR
Basingstoke and Oxford
Associated companies throughout the world

www.panmacmillan.co.uk/bello

ISBN 978-1-4472-5297-9 EPUB
ISBN 978-1-4472-8907-4 POD

Visit www.panmacmillan.com to read more about all our books
and to buy them. You will also find features, author interviews and
news of any author events, and you can sign up for e-newsletters
so that you're always first to hear about our new releases.

Chapter One

It was August. The weather was good and the men decided to start the harvest. The older children were not away at school yet. The work was all by hand and everyone was needed. Later the teacher and his wife came to help. Other islands in the group were using machines to do the harvest, but Kinness was still using the old ways. There *was* a tractor. Alec had a tractor and they used that to carry the hay from the fields to the crofts. They worked on each person's land in turn, starting at the south of the island. Everyone, except the very young and infirm, was helping. Mothers brought their children with them. A baby slept in a pram in the sun, toddlers played at the edge of the field. At midday they all ate together outside, where they were working. The islanders were not poor, but the harvest was always done this way.

They worked quickly while the weather lasted. It was unusual to have such a long spell of good weather. Storms could come quickly, without warning, and the harvest could be ruined. They wanted it finished by the time Jim brought his bride back in September. Some of them were going south for the wedding. So they worked quickly, and for a while the rhythm of the harvest—the bending to gather the hay to tie into stooks, the collection of the stooks together to dry and the movement of the tractor from field to croft—ruled the island.

Sarah wanted to get to the island as quickly as possible.

"Why bother with a honeymoon?" she said as they were planning the wedding. "Why not go straight to the island? We'll have our honeymoon there."

"There'll be no chance for a honeymoon once we're there," Jim said, and they decided on Cornwall.

Sarah had never been to Kinness. She had arranged to go once, to see it and meet Jim's family, but then her father had been ill and she was forced to cancel the trip.

She was quite determined, though, that they should live there once they were married. Where else would they live?

When she first met Jim he was working as assistant manager on a big farm in Cheshire and she was a student midwife in Liverpool. They had met at a party in the rugby club where her brother was a member. Jim had just joined and seemed detached from the rowdy good temper of the other young men. It seemed to Sarah that he was more mature than they were, but a little lonely. He treated her with old-fashioned politeness. In those first few months of their relationship he drank a good deal, but gave nothing of himself away. This aroused Sarah's curiosity and presented something of a challenge. She had just attended a course in psychiatry and thought that he was repressed.

He had not told her at first where he came from. She was English and did not recognize his accent. Later she was grateful for that. She would not have known, if he had told her, whether she was attracted to him or to the romantic idea that he belonged to the island. By the time he told her where he had spent his childhood she was convinced that she loved him. She had heard of the island because it had been featured in one of the colour magazines of a Sunday newspaper. The pictures of the crofts and the cliffs, the detailed description of the life there had caught her imagination. She especially remembered the faces, wary and cheerful, which stared out of the pages at her. The piece had been called "A Study of Paradise."

She was surprised when he asked her to marry him. He had become more relaxed with her, laughed more easily, and there had been moments of passion, though he seemed almost apologetic about them afterwards. But there had been no intimacy. She did not feel that she knew him. He told her that a croft had become vacant on Kinness and that it had been offered to him.

"But we would not need to live on the island," he said. "It might be better not to live there."

"But you love it," she said. "I can tell from the way you talk about it. You wouldn't be happy anywhere else."

This was wishful thinking. She could not tell what he thought about the island, because he hardly ever talked about it. She thought his reluctance to move back was on her behalf.

She enjoyed the honeymoon, but all the time they were in Cornwall she was thinking about moving to the island.

"Make the most of this," Jim said. "You'll be there soon enough."

But she pestered him to tell her about it, to describe the people and the house where they would live, and to go over the plans for the journey, until he was quite irritated.

"You'll be there soon enough," he repeated.

Eventually they were almost there. They drove north and took the overnight ferry to Baltasay, the biggest island in the group. The car was packed with their things. Other belongings had been sent on ahead. They took a cabin on the ferry, but Sarah did not sleep well. She was too excited. She had been looking forward to this for so long. She wished that she could share her excitement with Jim but he slept on the bunk above her and did not answer when she called out his name. The ferry pulled into the harbour on Baltasay very early in the morning. It was just as she had imagined. The harbour was full of fishing boats and gulls and the grey and white houses were crowded together around the water. The streets were narrow and cobbled.

Jim stood by her on the deck and pointed things out to her—his old school and houses where friends had lived. She was sure that he was pleased to be back.

They had breakfast in a café overlooking the harbour, then drove to the south of Baltasay to catch the boat to Kinness. Once they were out of the town the landscape was bleak and windswept. There were no trees, even around the crofts, and there were black scars in the hillside caused by peat digging. The road was new and good. They came upon occasional pockets of development—an enormous oil terminal and a modern concrete housing estate which looked like a prison. She tried to persuade herself that she was glad it was so bleak and so strange, and that made the trip even more exciting, but she felt disturbed and a little frightened.

The boat—the *Ruth Isabella*—belonged on Kinness and came to Baltasay once a week for mail, provisions, and passengers. Its base on Baltasay was a deep bay called Lutwick. There was a jetty there, but nothing more. Sarah had expected a village, more grey and white houses, perhaps a hotel where they could wait in comfort, but found only a corrugated iron shack, a telephone box, and a pebble beach. They were the first people to arrive at Lutwick. Later, when the boat appeared on the horizon, a mail van came down the road and parked by the hut, and then an old lady driving a delivery van with fresh meat, fruit, and vegetables. Inside the hut a tray of bread stood next to some of their furniture which had already been delivered. On the jetty there were drums of diesel and Calor Gas cylinders.

The boat seemed to approach very quickly and Sarah's high spirits returned. Baltasay might be bleak and ugly, but Kinness would be different. Hadn't the newspaper said that it was paradise? As the *Ruth Isabella* drew nearer the clouds parted and the sun came out. Sarah put her hand to her eyes to shield them from the reflected glare. Soon she could see every detail on the boat. Someone came out of the wheelhouse on to the deck and waved.

The old lady got out of the van and began to unload the goods inside it. The skin on her face was as tough and red as that of an old swede. The postman did not move and she began to complain to him about how heavy the boxes were, but he did not take the hint and get out to help her. He wound down the window of the van and looked out at the boat. The old woman nodded at Sarah, who was standing some distance away.

"That'll be Sandy Stennet's new daughter-in-law then," she said to the postman.

He grunted in reply.

"I think it's terrible sad for a young girl like that to be stuck on Kinness. Especially coming from the south, you'd think she'd want more from life than that."

"I went there once." The man spoke after a pause which gave the impression of considerable thought. "I didn't think a great deal of it."

"They say that they're terrible inbred," she said, inviting gossip.

But the postman had made his contribution. He climbed slowly out of his van and swung two sacks of letters behind him, without bothering to answer.

The boat was pulling into the jetty. A middle-aged man was at the wheel and two younger ones were acting as crew. The three men obviously belonged to the same family. Jim went forward to help. He took the ropes thrown by the younger men and made them secure. He shouted to them. They were laughing together. Sarah watched Jim throw back his head and laugh. She had never seen him like that before. He seemed to have become a different person. She did not understand what the men said to each other. The dialect they used was very broad and Jim had lapsed into it, too. For a moment she felt excluded and resentful. It was her day. She had expected to be the focus of attention. Why had Jim not introduced her?

Then Sarah recognized the three men. They had been at the wedding. The older man was Jim's father and the younger ones were his brothers. Alec was older than Jim. He was married and had two sons. Will was in the sixth form of the school at Baltasay. They came ashore. The father, Sandy, approached her, took her hands in his and kissed her. His face was brown and whiskery and smelled of oil and tobacco. She felt that Alec was staring at her. She looked at him and he winked at her and grinned. Will seemed embarrassed and looked away.

They loaded the boat efficiently and quickly. The postman drove back up the road, but the old woman waited in her van to watch. She seemed in no hurry to go. There would have been room to take Jim's car on the boat, but he had decided to leave it behind, for the time being at least. A friend would take it back to the town.

"The road's not very good on the island," he said. "It really needs improving. That's something I'll want to sort out."

Sarah rather liked the idea of a place with no cars and dilapidated roads. It was something else to make the island different.

"Surely we won't need a car," she said, but he took no notice.

The boat was loaded. Alec took Sarah by the hand and helped her aboard. He held her hand slightly longer than necessary. They were ready to go, but nothing happened. She wondered what they were waiting for. Alec had folded a rug for her, to sit more comfortably on the deck. She was sitting out of the wind and the sun felt quite warm on her face. Jim was in the wheelhouse with the other men. She could hear them talking and joking. She did not feel able to interrupt them to ask why they were waiting. The old woman with the grocery van must have decided that nothing more interesting was going to happen. Sarah watched her drive away. As she followed the van shaking up the narrow road away from Lutwick, she saw another car coming in the other direction. The men must have recognized it because they moved out of the wheelhouse and a prepared to cast off.

"Who is it?" Sarah asked. "What are we waiting for?"

"It's the taxi from town," Jim said. "We're expecting a passenger. He's been to the island several times. He's staying at the school house with Jonathan and Sylvia Drysdale."

Sarah watched the new arrival with a sense of superiority, because she belonged on the island now, although she had never been there and he was only a holidaymaker. She was disappointed when Sandy greeted the man even more affectionately than he had welcomed her. Even Jim seemed to consider him a friend. The passenger was perhaps in his midsixties. He was tall and gaunt, with a long forehead and long chin. His hair was very short. He was soberly dressed and his voice when he spoke to Sandy was well-bred English. He climbed easily aboard, and apologised immediately for being late. He seemed really to mind that he had kept them waiting. The taxi had broken down, he said, and it had taken a while to get it going again. Sandy reassured him that there was no hurry, but as soon as the man was settled next to Sarah, he started the engine. Will loosened the ropes and jumped aboard.

As the boat left the shelter of the Bay of Lutwick the breeze was stronger. The sun was bright, already low in the sky.

I should remember this, Sarah thought, every detail of it. This journey to Kinness seemed much more important to her than her marriage ceremony.

"You are very lucky to have the opportunity to live on the island," the man said to her, interrupting her thoughts, seeming to guess what she was thinking. "Sandy writes to me occasionally to keep me in touch with what is going on. He told me about you. Naturally he is delighted."

"Do you go to Kinness often?" she asked.

"Not as often as I would like. Jonathan, who teaches in the island primary school, was at university with my son. Jonathan shares my interest in ornithology and invited me to stay with him. You're not a birdwatcher are you?"

She shook her head.

"What a shame. Kinness is very good, you know, but it's desperately underwatched. I think it would rival Fair Isle if it were properly covered."

She did not know what he was talking about. She wanted to savour every moment of her journey to Kinness and did not ask him to explain.

It took nearly three hours to get there. Sarah wanted to capture the essence of it in her memory. She knew that she would never again feel such anticipation and excitement. But after the first sharp pleasure as the boat moved away from the jetty and she thought: this is it, the start of a new life for Jim and me, she became only sleepy and a little sick. The long monotonous rolls of the boat, and the sound of the engine and the meaningless jumble of words in the wheelhouse, made her drowsy. She did not quite sleep, but she closed her eyes and thought of nothing but the movement and sound of the boat, and the increasing sense of sickness in the pit of her stomach.

She was surprised when Jim came to tell her that they were nearly there. She had almost forgotten about him. As they approached the island the swell flattened and she felt ready to take an interest in her surroundings again.

"You weren't sick then," he said. "I thought that you might be sick."

"Not me," she said. "I'm an islander now, don't forget."

"There are lots of folk from the island who get seasick."

She took his hand to claim him again and to reassure herself that he belonged to her, not to the men in the wheelhouse. She made him sit by her and point out the features of the island. He began in a distant, dutiful way, but became more involved as the boat moved closer to the cliffs. She had seen a map of Kinness and knew its shape. They were approaching it from the north-east. It was roughly egg-shaped but tilted, with the longest part running north-east to south-west. The only natural harbour was on the west side—a small bay sheltered by two points. The boat would go down the north-east length of the island, round Ellie's Head, a round, high headland, and halfway up the west side to the harbour. Kinness was three miles long and two miles wide.

She stood up and leaned against the deck rail to get a first close view. The wind blew the spray on to her face. She took Jim's arm and pulled him close to her. He had a name for every cliff and valley and field. The north of the island was high and hilly, used only for grazing and peat. There were no crofts there, and the lighthouse which could be seen from Baltasay was automatic.

"The light was only made automatic about five years ago," Jim said. "Before that lighthouse men from the Northern Lights Board lived there with their families. My uncle was assistant keeper and used to cycle up the island for his watches. It was great fun to go with him."

He pointed out the cliffs where he had collected gulls' eggs, and where the puffins bred, and the hill where he and his family always dug their peat. She listened to the enthusiasm in his voice and thought: it was right for us to come back here to live although he pretended that he wasn't sure if he wanted to. He loves it.

He described the Hill Sheep Gather when they collected all the sheep for shearing, and showed her the seals hauled up on to the rocks at the base of the cliff. It was all she had dreamed of.

The land began to flatten and she saw the church and the school and low stone houses. At the very south of the island, above a rocky beach, he showed her the white house which would be their home. Then the *Ruth Isabella* moved north again and around one of the long curved headlands which protected the harbour from westerly gales, and Jim disappeared to help to bring the boat alongside the quay.

She had hoped that the islanders would do something special to mark her arrival, but it was all much more spectacular than she had imagined. She did not know that most of the islanders came to the harbour every boat day, and she thought that the whole of Kinness had turned out just to welcome her. There was a crowd and they all seemed to be waving and smiling. A banner reading JIM AND SARAH WELCOME HOME had been strung along the wall by the jetty. She felt like visiting royalty.

The other passenger tactfully left the boat first, quietly with no fuss, and disappeared into the crowd. Sarah stood, savouring the attention, the magic of being there, and waited for Jim to join her. He jumped on to the quay first. Instead of giving her his hand to help her ashore as she had expected, he took her into his arms and swung her on to the quay. The crowd cheered.

Other men went on to the boat then, and started to unload it. Sarah expected Jim to go with them to help, but he took her hand and led her off to introduce her to family and friends. She had met his immediate family at the wedding, but everyone wanted to take her hand, kiss her cheek. Jim stood close beside her, as if she might need protection from those people who only wanted to be friendly.

George Palmer-Jones, the elderly passenger, stood at the back of the crowd and watched with interest. He could not decide whether Sarah would settle on the island or not. He rather thought that she would not. He watched as Agnes, Jim's mother, tried to introduce her youngest child to Sarah. The child, Mary, would not have it. She pulled away from her mother's hand and would not look at

Sarah. George thought that Mary was playing up on purpose because she knew that Agnes would be specially upset if there was a scene today. The girl's face was red with the exertion of the tantrum, but she had a gleam in her eye as if she were enjoying herself immensely. Mary was twelve, but she behaved at times like a six-year-old. George thought that she was disturbed, but not as disturbed as she pretended to be. Perhaps if her deafness had been recognized earlier, or if Agnes had agreed to send her to a special school on the mainland, she might have been different.

"Come to meet your new sister-in-law," Agnes said. She spoke very slowly and looked directly at Mary so that the girl could lipread. "This is Sarah, Jim's wife."

"Don't want to!" Mary said. It seemed to George that she emphasised the nasal, toneless quality of the voice. She was exaggerating her deafness.

She hid behind her mother and began to kick and scream. Sarah did not know how to react to the girl's rudeness. She did not want her first day on the island spoilt by unpleasantness. She wished that Agnes would take Mary away. She was confident that she would win Mary round if she had the girl to herself. She was good with children. She had enjoyed her spell on the paediatric ward. She wanted children of her own. Lots of them. Of course her children would not be difficult or deaf.

She smiled at Agnes.

"Don't upset her," she said. "There will be plenty of time for Mary and I to become friends. I'm sure that we will be."

Behind her mother's back, Mary was sticking out her tongue and rolling her eyes, but Sarah pretended not to notice.

When Sarah moved on to greet another group of islanders, Mary left her mother and ran along the quay to where George Palmer-Jones was standing. He was nervous of her unpredictable behaviour, but during his holidays on Kinness she seemed to have become attached to him and his wife. She always came to the school house to visit them at least once during their stay. He usually left his wife to deal with the child and now he did not know what to say.

"That's a very pretty scarf you're wearing, Mary," he said. It was pretty. It was green silk with a batik pattern in black and white. "Where did you get it?"

She understood him immediately.

"It's a secret," she said. Then, after a pause: "Do you like secrets?"

"Very much."

"So do I. Will you be at the party tonight?"

"Yes."

"Will you dance with me? Nobody else will, except Daddy."

"Of course."

"I've another secret too. I'll tell it you at the party. I want to see Uncle James with the lorry."

She was gone. She ran down the road which led to her home, without waiting for her family, long legs and pigtails flying, the green silk scarf streaming behind her like a banner.

The men had finished unloading the boat. The diesel, gas, and provisions were stacked on the tractor and trailer. Jonathan Drysdale, the teacher, had been working with them. He left the other men, without a word, and joined George Palmer-Jones.

"Sorry to keep you waiting," he said. "We'll have to hang around a bit longer if you don't mind, until James comes with the lorry to take away the newlyweds. It's all nonsense but I've been told by some upstart in the Education department in Baltasay that I should participate more in community affairs."

They did not have long to wait. The lorry was big and very old. It had once been a coal lorry on the mainland. It had been on the island since Palmer-Jones had begun to visit. When it came down the hill to the quay now, driven by Jim's uncle James, George could see that it had been transformed into a vehicle of magnificence. There were heart-shaped balloons tied to the cab and the whole base of the lorry was covered in pink and white paper flowers. There was a throne of flowers for the couple to sit on, and their names were sprayed in silver paint on the bonnet. It had become a carnival float of a lorry.

How embarrassing! thought George Palmer-Jones as the young people were carried on to the lorry. But the girl's loving it. I hope that she doesn't expect it to be like this always.

"I'm sorry about all this," Jim said to Sarah. "I didn't expect quite so much fuss."

"It's lovely," she said.

It's over the top, Jim thought. They never did this when Alec brought Maggie back to the island. What are they trying to do? Then he saw a face in the crowd which he recognized. She's here, he thought. I didn't see her before. She must have been avoiding me. No one told me that she was here. So that's why they're making so much fuss. It's their way of saying sorry.

The lorry pulled away to take them home. Small children in their Sunday-best jerseys ran beside it and cheered. Sarah threw paper flowers to them and released the balloons.

Chapter Two

When the lorry disappeared over the horizon, the people at the quay began to disperse. Most of them walked home. The tractor and trailer would deliver most of the goods, then end up at Kenneth Dance's post office and stores. He would sort the mail and deliver it later. An old man and his sheep dog perched on the back of the trailer to get a lift down the island. The women and children walked back slowly together. The children were excited and dragged the balloons on strings behind them, but it was the same as every boat day. The women were talking about the preparation for the wedding party, but there were dances and parties throughout the autumn. The unloading of the boat had taken longer than usual—the sun was already low behind Ellie's Head—but with the disappearance of the lorry and the new arrivals everything had returned to normal.

James stopped outside Unsta—their new home—but did not leave the lorry, and drove away at once. The house stood above a pebble beach which Jim called the Haven. There was a small garden in the front surrounded by a drystone wall. A bench made from driftwood stood against the whitewashed wall of the house. There was a storm porch in the middle of the house, with doors on either side.

"That's in case of a gale," Jim said. "You'd never be able to open a door straight into the wind."

She waited outside for a moment, hoping that he might carry her in, but he seemed not to think of it. Perhaps lifting her on to the island from the boat had served the same purpose for him. She followed him into the house. It was small.

"There's no bathroom," he said immediately. "I explained to you that there's no bathroom."

"That's all right," she said. "Really it's no problem."

"If we decide to stay I can build one."

"Of course we'll decide to stay."

The front door led into a narrow passage. There were only two rooms. On one side was the bedroom and on the other the kitchen, with a small scullery at the back. In the kitchen there was a range. The fire was ready to light. Sarah suddenly felt chilled, and tried not to shiver. There was a little essential furniture in the room—a kitchen table, a couple of chairs—but it looked cold and bare.

"Alec and Maggie gave us this," Jim said. "For the time being. The old man who was here moved to the mainland to live with his sister and he took everything with him. Alec will bring our things on the tractor and trailer later."

"It'll be fun to start from scratch."

Everything was spotlessly clean, but the net curtains which hung at the windows were frayed and tatty, and the lino had lost all its colour.

"It's lovely," she said. "Really. It's lovely."

He took her hand and led her towards the bedroom. He stopped her at the door, picked her up, and carried her inside.

George and Jonathan walked back slowly to the school house. Jonathan had lingered at the quay, looking out at the gannets fishing over the sea until the islanders had gone. George felt awkward. He had made friends on Kinness and would have liked to walk down the island with them.

"How's Sylvia?" he asked

"Fine."

He had never found Jonathan easy to talk to. Every time he visited Kinness he felt that he was in the school house on sufferance. Drysdale was polite but George felt that the politeness was an effort. Yet each year the invitation came, and after he left there was a warm and friendly letter saying how much Jonathan and Sylvia enjoyed Palmer-Jones' visit.

"Did you have a good spring?" George asked.

Jonathan considered. "Not bad," he said in the end. "I broke my record for ringing auks. We didn't have any very special migrants."

He had a clipped, rather affected accent, which George found irritating. He must have been thirty-five but he still looked and sounded like a public-school boy. Molly, George's wife, thought that Jonathan was shy, but that had never seemed to George a reasonable excuse for rudeness.

"I've been invited to the party tonight," George said. "Sandy wrote to me specially. Will you and Sylvia be going?"

"We've been invited," he said. "Everyone on the island's been invited. I suppose that we'll have to go. Sylvia's very keen. And as I said, I've been told to participate in community affairs."

The school house was in the middle of the island. The classroom was in the same building. The house was grey, two-storeyed. They could see it from the road which wound round from the harbour. Nothing else broke the horizon. To the left of the road built into the hill, beyond a lochan smooth and round as a mirror, was Kell, the croft where James Stennet lived. It was immaculate, freshly whitewashed, with a neat pile of driftwood stacked by the back door. Then the road fell sharply past the low marshy area known as the Loons. In the spring it was covered with long grasses and flowers. Beyond that were the green folds of the clifftop and the sea. George forgot that Jonathan irritated him and enjoyed being on Kinness.

Sylvia had seen them coming and was at the door to meet them. For the first time since his arrival George felt welcome. She had long chestnut curls and a warm wide smile. There was tea made and hot scones and a fire in the grate in the living room.

"It is so nice to see you," Sylvia said, and she approached George to be kissed. Her hair smelled of the hot scones and the fire.

She led them into the living room. It was light, a mix of traditional island croft and modern comfort. Sylvia sat on a sheepskin rug by the fire and gestured the others to sit down.

"Isn't it lucky," she said, "that you could make it in time for the wedding party?"

She began to chat about the preparations for the evening. Jonathan got up and stood by the window. He said nothing.

Elspeth Dance sat in her parents' home at the post office with her son on her knee. They were in the kitchen. Kenneth was sorting the mail on the table. Anne was putting the final decorations on the cakes which she had promised for the party.

"No one has told him that I'm back," Elspeth said. "He was surprised to see me."

"Does it matter?" Kenneth said. "Surely not after all this time."

"It matters to me," Elspeth said. "Someone should have told him. He should have been given the choice."

"What choice? Do you really think it would have made any difference?"

"I don't know. We were so close."

Annie looked up from the cakes she was decorating meticulously.

"You're making too much of it," she said sternly. "It's all over. It was over years ago. Don't you go stirring it up again."

"Should I go to the party tonight then?"

"Of course you'll go. You mustn't disappoint Ben." Annie looked tenderly at her grandson.

"Do you think Jim knows what happened?" Elspeth sounded frightened.

"How could he know?"

"I'm warning you," Elspeth said. "There'll be trouble."

"Should I go over and see if they've everything they need?" Alec said.

"No. They've only been married a week. They surely want to be on their own. They've got everything they need. I've never seen such a fuss."

Maggie was sandy-haired and sensible. She had been an infant teacher on Baltasay before they married. They had been to school together. She had no illusions about Alec or about the island when she moved to Kinness. "We didn't have all that carry-on when we were wed," she said, with a touch of regret.

"Would you have wanted it? We had the party."

"I wouldn't have had it any different."

"Where are the boys?"

"In the garden playing. I'll bring them in right at the last minute to get them changed and ready. Otherwise they'll get dirty again."

"Do you think that they'll settle?"

"The boys?"

"No. Jim and Sarah."

"I expect so. Given time. We did. Why?"

"If they moved off there'd be nothing to stop me buying the Unsta land. We need more land if we're going to make any sort of living."

She had heard it all before.

"Your father managed and he has less land than us."

"Things have to change."

"Things will change. Sandy and Agnes won't be able to stay at Sandwick forever. Especially when Will goes. Then they'll need someone to work their land. But this isn't the time to discuss it with Jim. There'll be time enough for that."

"But what will happen when Mum and Dad do have to leave Sandwick? You know what's in the will. You know what arrangements will be made if they move somewhere smaller. They're besotted by that child. I want more land. You want a bigger house with more room for the boys. But I'm not prepared to pay their price to get it."

She thought that he still looked very young, much younger than her. He had very thick dark hair. His wasn't an island face. It was dark, southern, brooding.

"Let it be for tonight," she said. "It'll have to be sorted out, but not today."

He shrugged agreement.

"And behave yourself this evening. Don't have too much to drink. You always show yourself up."

He took no notice. No woman was going to tell him how to

behave. He went out into the yard to switch on the generator. His new tractor was there. It comforted him and encouraged him. Progress was possible on Kinness. He had proved it.

In Sandwick Will sat in his bedroom, keeping out of the way, until it was time to go to the party. Downstairs there was a muddle of preparation. His parents were always so disorganized, he thought with intolerance. Everything at Sandwick was so messy, chaotic. He would be glad to go back to school. He missed his friends, the conversations in the hostel late at night, his status as a sixth former. Here, the only debate was about sheep and fish. He wondered how the Drysdales, who had experience of more civilized ways, could stand it.

Outside in the passage he heard Mary screaming as Agnes tried to brush her hair.

Mother's so weak, he thought, listening to Agnes' fraught, ineffectual words, and so dependent on Dad. My wife will be independent, a person in her own right.

He picked up his guitar and began to play, humming a folk tune to the chords.

"I hate you," Mary was screaming. "I hate both of you."

I don't hate them, Will thought. They're kind and generous and I love them. But I can't spend the rest of my life here. It would kill me.

"But you must come," James said. "You promised." His head was thundering with tension, anger, and compassion. "You'll enjoy it."

"I would have enjoyed it once," Melissa said. She took his hand and tried to make her voice sound reasonable. She had been an actress once. She tried to recall the skill, but knew that she sounded shrill and unnatural.

"Look," she said. "I have tried. I did want to come. But you can't understand the panic, when I think of all those people in the hall. I can't face it. They won't miss me."

He gave in immediately. He knew that there was no point in trying to persuade her. At first he had been sympathetic about her moods and depressions. There had been cause enough. Miscarriage after miscarriage. And she had been so desperate for a child. But that had been years ago.

She had not come from Kinness, not from any of the other islands. That had been part of the problem. When he first met her she had not seemed to have come from anywhere. She was getting off the big boat at the harbour on Baltasay. He was on his way home after National Service. She was very small and frail, wrapped up in a big coat. She had plenty of money.

"What brings you to the islands?" he had asked. She had been waiting on the quay, looking lost and unhappy. Her smallness and vulnerability had attracted him. The women on the island were strong and big-boned.

"I was expecting a friend," she had said. "He said that he'd meet me from the boat."

"Who would that be, then? I know most of the folk here. I used to anyway."

She had given the name of the owner of the only big hotel on Baltasay, an Englishman, who had appeared mysteriously after the war.

"That's no problem then," he said. "You can leave your bags with Jean in the harbour office and we'll walk. It isn't far."

The Englishman had been surprised to see her but had put on a good enough show of being pleased that she was there.

James had not been able to forget her. He had used every excuse to get to Baltasay to see her. He had dressed up in the suit which was too big for him and sat in the hotel bar waiting to catch a glimpse of her. Very often she was there before him. Sometimes the Englishman was with her, loud and showing her off to his friends. Usually she was on her own. She looked around her with big black eyes, made up in a way he had never seen before, staring out of her tiny white face. Then one night he had arrived at the hotel and she had been different. She was in her place at the bar but the smudges under her eyes were caused not by make-up but by tears.

"I've got to leave tomorrow," she said. "He's told me that I've got to go. He's found some other fancy woman." She never spoke of the Englishman by name.

"What will you do?"

"I don't know." She had never spoken of her past. She seemed to belong nowhere.

"Have you friends to go to? Family?"

"No."

"Come home with me. You know I would have asked you anyway if you'd been free. We'll be married." Then, as she hesitated: "Or I'll come with you. Wherever you like."

She had been his obsession. He had dreamed of touching her, of knowing her. While he waited for her to give her reply he thought that the whole thing was impossible. He had frightened her away.

"No," she had said at last. "I'll come with you. To Kinness."

At that time he had never kissed her. He had only touched her to take her arm on that first day, by the harbour, to take her to the hotel.

"And we will be married?"

"If that's what you want." It really had not mattered to her one way or the other.

They were married quietly on the island. There had been none of the fuss of balloons and flowers. They had been happy, intensely happy until, he thought, she began to crave for a child, in the same way as he craved for her.

She was still lovely. She still had the fine features and big, dark eyes.

"I'm sorry," she said. "I've let you down again."

"Don't be silly," he said.

She was sitting on a stool in the bedroom, in front of the dressing table mirror. He knelt behind her and put his arms around her, so that he was holding her tight against him. She let herself melt back into his body until he touched her breast. Then he felt her shrink away from him, though she tried not to do it. He stood up and started to get ready to go out alone, to the party.

Jim was woken by the sound of Alec's generator. Sarah was still asleep. He could hear her breathing and feel her hair on his cheek. She thought it would all be so easy. He had never meant to come back. He had always thought that the island men who went to the mainland for a spell to find themselves a wife were no better than Viking raiders. But she had tempted him with her enthusiasm. Perhaps he should never have listened to her. He looked at his watch and shook her gently.

"Hey. We'll have to get ready. Dad will be here in half an hour."

There were thin blue curtains at the window. She had drawn them before they went to bed. She wrapped herself in a blanket, went to the window, and looked out. It was dusk. The sun had gone but there was light enough to see the beach and the silhouettes of the upturned boats pulled up there.

Jim was pulling clothes from suitcases. She could not understand the urgency. She went up to him and kissed him.

"You can switch on the light," Jim said. "Alec's put on the generator. The light will work now."

She switched on the light and the magic of the beach and the grey sky disappeared.

"I'll heat some water for washing," Jim said. "Maggie said that your dress is in the wardrobe. They cleaned it for you. Apparently one of the seams had split. She got someone to mend it for you." He went into the kitchen.

It was the tradition to wear the wedding dress at the party. Sarah was so used to being married now, that it seemed odd to be dressing up again. But she wanted it to be right for everyone on the island. She wanted to be a beautiful bride for Jim. It was a white dress in a heavy cotton, with a square neck and a tight bodice. The skirt was long and full. There was broderie anglaise around the bottom of the skirt and at the cuffs of the tight sleeves. It had been beautifully laundered. All the pin tucks in the bodice had been carefully ironed.

She took the dress out of the wardrobe and laid it on the bed. As she did so she saw that there was a pin still in the hem. She lifted the skirt to take it out. It had not been used in mending the dress. It pinned a white square of paper to the cloth. She pulled it out, and read the words which had been written on it. The words said: He should have been mine.

She took no notice and threw the paper on to the bed. It meant nothing to her then.

Chapter Three

The hall had been decorated with streamers and more of the heart-shaped balloons. Maggie and Agnes had been there all morning, laying the tables, preparing food. Sandy arrived at the hall first. In Sandwick Agnes was still trying to calm Mary and herself, and he welcomed the peace of the empty hall. He helped himself to a glass of whisky. The women had made a fine job of preparing the hall. He would not let Jim down in front of his smart English bride. The room was arranged like a second wedding reception, with the tables set out in a traditional horseshoe shape. The bride and groom and immediate family would sit at the top table. There was another wedding cake. Everything would be done in the proper way.

Agnes arrived then with Mary and Will, and soon the other guests came in, stamping the mud from their shoes, calling out to each other as if they had not met for months. Sandy and Agnes greeted them as they arrived, handing out small glasses of whisky. Everyone was dressed up. The men wore dark, old-fashioned suits, the women their smartest dresses. Mary stood behind her parents. She, too, was neatly dressed but she still wore the green silk scarf which George had admired in the afternoon.

George Palmer-Jones followed the Drysdales into the hall. He had been put to sit with them at the end of one of the tables—a small group of outsiders. As they waited for Sarah and Jim, Sylvia gave him her full attention. Jonathan might not have been there. He felt flattered by her interest and found that he was putting into words ideas which he had discussed with no one else, not even his wife.

"How are you enjoying retirement?" Sylvia asked. "You seem to be busy."

"Yes. I'm always very busy, but not in a particularly satisfying way."

"What do you mean?"

He considered. "I think that I miss the structure, the discipline of work."

"Are you thinking of going back to work, then?" She smiled at him in a sympathetic, encouraging way. She was leaning over the table towards him, and the copper hair fell over her shoulders, so that he could see the bare, creamy skin at the back of her neck. He remembered his work as a civil servant in the Home Office, part administrator, part policeman.

"Not exactly. I was thinking of setting up on my own."

He was distracted by the smooth neck, the touch of her ankle against his leg. He would not otherwise have confided in her.

"How exciting! What as?"

"Oh," he said vaguely, "as a consultant. To provide an advisory service in my own field." Then, perhaps to impress her, he said: "It would make me a private detective, I suppose."

He had never used the words before and he thought how sleazy and squalid they sounded.

"How exciting!" she repeated, but she did not sound impressed and he thought she was thinking of something else. He turned away from her and watched Sandy and Agnes greet their guests by the door.

James came in alone. George had met Melissa once, quite by chance when she was out walking on the hill. He had hoped to see her again and was disappointed that James was alone. Poor Melissa, George thought. So she couldn't face it. James took a glass of whisky and drank it very fast. George was surprised. He was a lay preacher. He did not usually drink at all.

The guests all began to take their seats. The two families were separated as usual. The Dances sat on one side of the horseshoe and the Stennets on the other. Nothing was meant by the separation, but everyone felt more comfortable that way.

Sandy went out to tell the young couple that their guests were ready for them. It only took him five minutes to get from the hall to Unsta. As he went out of the door he put on the old cap which he always wore. He was happy. He had all his children home now. He had never lived off the island and could not understand the attraction of life away. There had been a real contentment in seeing everyone together in the hall to welcome Jim and his English wife. She would settle soon. The women would make her feel at home. Maggie was a good woman and would help her.

It was dark and there was only an occasional moon but he knew the road to Unsta well enough. It had been his father's house. He had been born there. He had built Sandwick after he had married Agnes. He had wanted his own place, his own land. I was ambitious too, he thought, when I was young. Alec is like me. But he is impatient. He has too many new ideas all at once. I have Mary to think about. She must come first. The others can look after themselves. Maggie is a good woman but she pushes Alec. He has ambition enough without her pushing him. I was lucky. Agnes was happy to leave the planning to me.

He arrived at Unsta. The curtains were drawn and he could not see in. He opened the porch door, and was just about to go into the house when he stopped and knocked. I have never had to knock on this door, he thought. Well, everything has to change.

Because he had knocked on the door for the first time, he saw and heard everything as if for the first time. An old oilskin was hanging in the porch and reminded him of fishing trips with his father. He heard the background sound of waves on shingle, and the chug of the generator from its shed at Buness over the lane.

The door opened and Jim stood there, scrubbed and spruce, with the light behind him.

"You didn't have to knock," Jim said. "Will you come in?"

"Better not," said his father. "They're all there now and waiting for you both. You know what they're like."

"Waiting to get at the food and the dancing."

Sandy nodded.

Sarah heard them talking.

"I'm just coming," she shouted. "I'm nearly ready."

She came out through the bedroom door and stood in the hall. Jim moved out of the doorway and into the darkness of the porch, so that both men could see her framed by the light. Her long hair was loose and she wore not a veil, but a white shawl of local lace pinned to her hair, which fell around her shoulders.

"Do I look all right?" she asked. "Will I do?"

"You'll do fine," Sandy said. "You'll do just fine."

He stepped into the house to take her hand, and she could see then that he was beaming. He looks like a furry animal, she thought, with his round face and round nose and big front teeth. She realized that he looked just like an illustration of Ratty in an edition of *Wind in the Willows* which she had loved as a child.

She took his arm and the three of them walked together up the road to the hall. It was on some high ground in the middle of the southern bulge of the island. Sarah could see it almost as soon as they left Unsta because of the long lit windows and the light outside its door. As they approached she could hear the talking and the laughing.

"I'm nervous," she said. "I never thought that I would be."

She had been talking to Jim, but Sandy replied.

"There's nothing to be afraid of," he said. "Not here on Kinness. You're home now. Besides, you don't have to do anything except look pretty."

They had arrived at the door of the hall. Although it had been a warm day, it was colder now, with the sharp clarity of autumn. They hesitated.

"What do we do now?" Sarah asked. She shivered. She was standing underneath the light fixed on the wall, and the shadow at her feet was strange and witchlike, because of the long dress and the shawl.

"Just give me a minute," Sandy said. "Then Jim knows what to do."

He took half a bottle of whisky from his pocket and took a swig, then pushed open the door into the hall. It swung back on a heavy spring almost immediately, before Sarah could see what was happening inside, but she felt a rush of warm air and she shivered again.

Inside, they must have been waiting for Sandy to come back, because they were quiet at once, and expectant. He must have been standing just inside the door, because when he spoke his voice was very loud.

"Ladies and gentlemen," he said, "can we welcome Sarah and Jim."

There was a sound of chairs scraping against a wooden floor as they all stood up, then the door was open and she was in there with them. Jim took her hand and they walked together around the room. The guests were clapping. After waiting outside in the darkness, the lights seemed very bright. The room was very warm. Sarah wished that it was all over. She had expected to enjoy the attention, but she was overawed by the strange faces and the noise and the staring eyes. She supposed that they were looking at Jim, too, but it seemed that everyone was staring at her critically and with interest. Eventually she reached her place at the table, but there were more cheers before Jim took his hand from her arm, and she was allowed to sit down.

Then the guests sat, too, and began talking to each other, so that they were no longer looking at her, and she began to relax a little. She looked down the table, avoiding curious eyes. There were plates of cold meat and dishes of vegetables for people to help themselves, thick cups and saucers and enormous institutional teapots. It was very different from the first wedding reception in the smart hotel in Chester, where the toasts were drunk in champagne, there was a professional photographer, and the waitresses were dressed in black.

Jim interrupted her thoughts. "You must start to eat," he whispered. "They're all desperate to get at the food, but they won't like to until you do."

She helped herself and immediately there was a clatter of spoons against china, plates and dishes were passed along the table, and the party began. As they ate she could look at the people more closely. They concentrated so hard on their plates and the

27

conversation that there was no danger that they would see her watching, return her stare. There were perhaps forty people, of all ages, in the room.

"Is everyone here?" she asked. "Everyone who lives on Kinness?"

"Everyone except Melissa."

"Melissa?"

"My uncle James' wife. She's not very strong. She doesn't get out much."

"That's sad. It would have been nice to have everyone here."

"Yes. It would have been nice."

"We'll save her some cake."

But he had begun to talk to Agnes who was sitting on the other side of him. He was teasing his mother, and his voice had slipped into the accent which Sarah could not understand. Throughout the meal and the speeches she felt isolated because of her imprecise understanding of the dialect. Usually she could guess at the meaning but then a word was used which was unclear and she was left feeling that she had gained the wrong impression of the whole thing, and so had reacted inappropriately. Will I speak like that one day? she thought, and she found the idea frightening. When I speak like that I won't be me any more. I'll be one of them, just another of the Kinness folk. Then she thought: my children will definitely speak like that, and unaccountably she found that idea reassuring.

After the meal, and the cups of tea, they drank toasts in whisky to the bride and the groom. She cut her second wedding cake. The plates were cleared and taken to the kitchen and they prepared for the speeches.

Sandy spoke first, simply and briefly.

"I have one beautiful daughter," he said, patting Mary's head. "Now I have two."

Alec had been Jim's best man. At the first reception his speech had been short and restrained. He had been ill at ease. Now be enjoyed himself with a raucous, bawdy performance which had his audience yelling and laughing at him. At first Sarah thought that she was not understanding properly, but there was no mistaking the suggestive gestures, the obvious crudeness of the jokes. Then she was angry as she watched him leaning against the table, his black hair greased away from his face in a conceited imitation of an ageing rock star. Why should I laugh? she thought. I wouldn't laugh at jokes like this at home. Why is he spoiling the evening for me?

Then he began to do an impersonation of Jim which was so real and so funny that she laughed too, despite herself, and found that she was clapping and cheering with the rest.

When Alec finished speaking they moved the tables and chairs to one side of the room. James played the fiddle, Kenneth Dance the accordion and Will the guitar.

"We'll have to dance first," Jim said.

"But I can't. Not this sort of dancing." She liked the idea of it but she did not want to make a fool of herself.

"It doesn't matter. They won't expect you to be able to."

They watched sympathetically as she muddled her way through the dance, then she sat down to watch. She had been taught Scottish dancing at school but this was quite different. The music was as crude and alive as Alec's voice had been, and the dancers moved with a supple, contained energy. The next dance was announced as an Eightsome Reel and Jim led Agnes on to the floor. He moved with the same tight-bottomed, flat-footed step as the other men. They danced in a square with three other couples. One of the sequences of moves involved the women dancing alone in the middle of the set while the others clapped. At first it was Agnes' turn, then a young woman, a little older than Sarah, took her place. She caught Sarah's attention because she was so self-conscious. She danced very well, but without the others' spontaneity.

Sarah turned to a short, old man, dressed in a shiny green-black suit, who was sitting next to her, clapping to the rhythm of the music.

"Excuse me," she said. "Who is that woman? The one who's dancing now."

"That's Elspeth," he answered. "Elspeth Dance." He grinned mischievously. "We did all think at one time that her and your Jim would be married. There was some that was against it, but I thought that it would be a good thing. They didn't take any notice of me. They never do."

He smiled at her again. He seemed not to mind that no notice was taken of his opinion or to realize that he might be giving offence. She did not know what to say, but he did not expect an answer. The Eightsome Reel was coming to an end.

"Will you dance with me?" he asked eagerly.

"I'm sorry. I don't know how."

"Jim must teach you," he said. "We have lots of socials. I'd like to dance with you."

He went off to find another partner. She saw that he walked with a limp. The reel had finished. She watched Jim. He came straight towards her, without exchanging a word with Elspeth. He stood by Sarah's side, watching the dancers. He did not speak.

"I was talking to that old man," Sarah said, "he seems quite a character."

"Robert? You should take no notice of what he says. He's an old fool."

He realized that he had spoken sharply. He took her hand. "We have to get the Cup," he said, more gently, he took her into the small kitchen at the back of the hall. Maggie was there, stirring a pan which stood on one of the two gas rings.

"It's ready," she said. "Do you want to taste it?"

"Why not?"

She ladled some of the hot liquid into a teacup. Jim sipped at it, then handed it to Sarah. She tasted it. It was hot, spicy, and very alcoholic.

"It's delicious. What is it?"

She drank the remainder.

"It's a secret recipe," Jim said. "Mother made it. She'll pass the recipe to you when our children are old enough to marry. It's another tradition."

"I think it's unhygienic," Maggie said. "Everyone drinking out of the same old bowl. Take care that the children don't get at it."

"It's the Cup," Jim said. Sarah could not tell whether his reverence was genuine or mocking. It was on the table: a large silver bowl with a handle at each side. "No one knows when it first came to Kinness. There are all sorts of legends. It's used at every wedding. We take it round to share a drink with every guest. It's supposed to bring us luck."

Soon after Sarah realized that she was drunk. Later she was to remember the evening as a series of events brought suddenly into sharp focus, and the rest, even the time before she started to drink from the Cup, was a blur of loud music and dancing people. It was like a peculiar game of musical statues, except that often, at her times of clarity, the music continued.

So, she retained an image of Alec giving his best man's speech, leering at the guests across a laden table as he described in graphic detail what he had wished for Jim and his new wife.

She remembered Jim dancing the Eightsome Reel, poised like an African warrior with his pulled-in buttocks and bent knees, but moving only to take a woman in his arms, the woman whom everyone thought he should marry.

She remembered seeing that woman later as they went round the room with the Cup. She had a picture of Elspeth Dance standing like a statue, staring at them with blue eyes as they approached her with the drink, and remembered the conversation between Jim and Elspeth as though it were taking place a long way off.

"Hello Elspeth," her husband said. "I didn't realize that you were back."

"I thought that you were surprised to see me."

"How long have you been home?"

"Not long. I don't know whether I shall stay. I'm not committed to anything."

Sarah thought that she must have been introduced to Elspeth and that they had drunk together from the Cup, but that was all part of the blur.

There was another image of Mary, dancing with Robert, the old man. Despite his limp he was keeping up with her and they were laughing together.

And another of Elspeth, standing on the stage, singing

unaccompanied while the band rested. She had a deep and husky voice, and she sang a love song.

The next thing she remembered was being outside. She was alone. She was leaning for some reason against a gravestone. It was covered with furry lichen which she was touching with her finger. The sky was clear now and the stars whirled around her with the same violence as the dancing people in the hall. She felt sick and sat down. She could hear the voices in the hall, and the sea, and it occured to her that all the people for miles and miles were in the hall. She alone was outside, under the whirling stars. Except Melissa, she thought. She's not there. And then, to spoil the image altogether, she heard the sound of running-footsteps. Then the door opened and she heard a couple of women shouting goodnight, calling that they had to get the bairns home to bed.

She had nothing more to drink. She went back into the hall and joined the dancing. It did not seem to matter now that she did not know the steps.

The last of the still and vivid pictures which she retained forever, and which sobered her, was of Agnes crying. Sarah went to find Jim. The family were gathered around Agnes, trying to comfort her, but she was shouting at them.

"What's the matter?" Sarah asked Jim.

"It's Mary," Jim said. "It seems that she's gone missing. I expect she's back at Sandwick. Sandy's gone to look."

But she was not at Sandwick and there was no more dancing.

George Palmer-Jones could not enter into the spirit of the celebration. He had been to parties on Kinness before and had always enjoyed them, but tonight he found the earthy speeches, the boisterous contact, strangely shocking.

How pagan they are still, he thought, as Alec swung his partner about him, exposing a layer of underskirt and a stockinged leg. They pretend to be Christian, but when they've had a few drinks, they still behave like loutish Norsemen.

He wondered how much of his disenchantment was caused by his lack of decision over his future. He had retired. Why should he again put himself into a position when his time was not his own? How could lie indulge in? his passion for ornithology if someone else was paying him to work for them? He was determined that he would come to a decision by the end of the holiday, and seemed unable to put the problem from his mind.

Sylvia got up to dance with Sandy. She smiled at George as she made her way on to the floor. He took no notice of her. He knew that she wanted him to dance with her and that she thought he was being unfriendly. Let her think what she liked. If she wanted to make a spectacle of herself that was her business. He preferred to be a little dignified.

The chairs and tables had been moved to the sides of the room to prepare for the dancing, and he sat, squashed in a comer by a pile of coats. He was still sitting there when Mary found him. She held by the hand a thin, pale boy of about six or seven.

"This is Ben," Mary said. "He's come to stay on the island, at the post office. His mummy's called Elspeth."

George said unconvincingly that he was pleased to meet Ben.

"I can't tell you my secret yet," she said. "It wouldn't be a secret if Ben heard it, and he doesn't like being on his own. You haven't forgotten that you promised to dance with me?"

"No," he said. "I haven't forgotten. I'll dance with you later. Not now though."

She seemed satisfied with that and dragged Ben away.

Suddenly George felt irritated by his own churlishness and he stood up. He went to sit by Jonathan Drysdale, the only other guest who seemed not to be participating with any pretence of enjoyment. Sylvia was dancing now with Kenneth Dance, and was moving as deftly and gracefully as any of the island women. The two men watched her for a moment. She knew that she was being watched, and enjoyed it.

"You don't dance, then?" George asked, for something to say.

"No. I don't seem to be able to get the hang of it."

"Sylvia's very good."

"Yes." He seemed please by the compliment to his wife, then said: "She says that there's nothing else to do here."

"She's not happy on Kinness?"

"She was at first. She was the one who was most keen to live here. She's always been very interested in crafts. That was her subject. At art school. She had all sorts of notions of having a small workshop, perhaps with a loom, doing her own spinning and dyeing, but it never came off."

"Why was that?"

"I'm not quite sure. There were a lot of obstacles. The islanders were very wary of outsiders. That was seven years ago, and they were even more narrow-minded then than they are now. They thought that we were wicked because we wouldn't go to church. Things have changed a bit. At first I thought Maggie was quite enlightened. She had a few new ideas, and because she was one of the family they had to listen to her. But even she's caused problems lately. It's hard going at times."

"Have you thought of leaving?"

"Yes, of course I've considered it. But I'm in the middle of a study of the black guillemots." For the first time since he had arrived on the island George saw Drysdale show some animation. "I'll need at least another two years to get any meaningful data. It would be lunacy to go now."

"But Sylvia wants to leave?"

Jonathan shrugged.

"She's bored," he said. "I don't think she likes to admit it. She was so excited about coming but if I got another job she would be immensely relieved."

It was not until the Cup had been passed several times around the room that Palmer-Jones remembered his promises to Mary.

He looked over the floor. Most of the dancers seemed to be drunk. Sarah was stumbling through a dance with Jim. They were both laughing. Her white dress was grubby at the hem, and she had taken off her shoes and was moving in bare feet. Sylvia was giggling, trying to drag Jonathan to his feet to join her. George felt pompous and straight-laced.

The band stopped then. There was a break in the proceedings and more home-made cakes and scones and biscuits were laid out on the table at the back of the room. George thought that perhaps Mary had been helping to prepare the food in the kitchen and he went to find Maggie.

"Have you seen Mary?"

"No. Little madam. She was supposed to be giving me a hand. What that child needs is a spanked bottom."

Her freckled face was red with exertion and her sandy hair seemed to have lost its perm. George realized that he had not seen Maggie dancing.

"It must have been hard work," he said, "organizing all this. Not much fun being stuck in the kitchen all evening."

"Oh well," she said. "I don't mind. At least I wouldn't mind if it was appreciated. But Sandy and Agnes spend so much time bothering about that spoilt brat that they don't get round to considering other folks."

"So you don't know where Mary is?"

"She'll be hiding somewhere. She does that quite often when she's after attention."

So he thought no more of it, and enjoyed Elspeth's singing.

Agnes had been drinking from the Cup, too, so it took her longer than it would otherwise have done to realize Mary was missing. She had told the girl to go to Maggie to help prepare the supper, but that had been a while before the interval. While they ate and while Elspeth was singing she presumed that Mary was in the kitchen. She congratulated herself even, that her daughter had obeyed her. There was a lot of coming and going. Some of the women were taking younger children home to bed, and the men went outside to drink from illicit bottles of whisky and relieve themselves.

But later, when the dancing started again, and Maggie joined them and asked angrily why Mary had not been in to help, she began to get anxious. She began to ask if anyone had seen the girl, shouting to be heard above the music. When no one could tell her where Mary was, she went to find Alec. He was dancing with Sylvia Drysdale. It was a waltz and he was holding her very close, but Agnes did not notice that.

"Mary is missing," she said, prodding his back to get his attention.

"You must go and look for her. I will tell your father. You must both go."

"Mother," he said, yelling with exasperation and to make sure that he was heard. "She's always going missing when no one's taking any notice of her. I'm not spoiling my evening to play her silly games."

It was then that Agnes began to cry.

"You don't care about her," she sobbed. "You've never cared for her. She's my daughter and I'm proud of her. I love her. You don't understand. She needs all of your help, but you don't understand."

They gathered around her. They thought that it was the drink that made her maudlin. "She's not used to it," they said. But because of who she was they humoured her. Sandy went to Sandwick to see if Mary was there. When he returned to say that she was not, the party broke up. They began to search the island.

Kell was the northernmost croft on the island. It was a mile from the nearest house. At the back of the house rose the mountain where the skuas seemed to fight with sheep for land. The back of the house was always dark.

Melissa sat in the kitchen. She was remembering the dance they had on the island when she came with James. They had been married on the island. They had been married in the church. She had told him that she had no faith but he said that it did not matter. Everyone was married in church. He did not believe her when she said that she had no family to invite, but he did not press her.

Sandy and Agnes had been married just a few years before and were very happy and lighthearted. They had made her feel welcome and wanted. They had been great friends, the four of them. Later she and Agnes had become pregnant at the same time, and when she lost the baby Agnes had been the person who had given the most comfort. It pleased her to know that life continued, and her sister-in-law's swelling belly was a sign of hope that she, too, could carry a baby again. But although there were other pregnancies none of the babies survived and as Agnes' family grew, Melissa became bitter and distant.

She knew that she needed help. But who on Kinness could give it? There was an elderly nurse, a spinster, who played the organ in the church and taught the children in Sunday school. Could she go to her and say:

"Help me. I can't bear my husband to touch me"?

The nurse had never been touched, seemed to know nothing of frustration or desire.

In England there would be places to go, people to see—sympathetic doctors, marriage guidance counsellors. Once, a long time ago, she had suggested to James that she should go south to seek advice, but he had been hurt.

"I can look after you," he had said. "I can care for you. You don't need other people."

Now he would be glad for her to go, but it was too late. She was frightened to go to the south of the island where most of the houses were gathered. How could she get on an aeroplane and go to England?

I'm ill, she thought. I live too much in the past.

She heard the door of the storm porch banging. She hoped that it was the wind but she knew it was James.

He was still holding the powerful torch he had been using to search for Mary. She blinked and covered her eyes with her hands.

"What are you doing, sitting here in the dark?" he said. As usual irritation and concern were mixed. "The engine's still on, you could have put the light on. Besides, it's very late. You should be in bed."

"Yes. I didn't notice the time."

She's getting worse, he thought, I must do something, get a specialist from the mainland maybe. But the last doctor from the mainland had given her tranquillizers and she had not taken them.

She stood up. She was wearing a dressing gown and as she stood up it fell open, so that he could see her neck and the top of her breast. Her skin looked very white in the light of the torch.

She saw him looking at her.

"I'm sorry," she said.

"I'm off out again," he said. "I've just come in to get changed into warmer clothes. Mary is missing. I doubt if she's strayed this far up the island, but I said I'd look on the mountain. Don't wait up or me. It'll take a while."

But he was still looking at her.

"I love you," he said.

As he walked out of the door, and the chill air hit him, he thought: it's not love I feel for her. It's lust. Then he thought: there are worse sins than lust, and he went out onto the island.

Chapter Four

When Sarah woke the bedroom was bright with sunshine. She had a hangover. At the instant of waking she thought that she was still in Cornwall. The clarity of the light was the same. Then she felt the headache and remembered where she was. She stretched. She supposed that there was no hurry to get up but she wanted to explore the island. She wondered if Jim had made any tea. There was no noise in the kitchen. She got out of bed and put on a thick jersey on top of her nightdress. The lino felt cold on her feet. There was no one in the kitchen. She plugged in the electric kettle to make tea but there was no electricity. The fire in the range was out and the grate had not been cleaned. How thoughtless of Jim to go out so early without showing her how to light the fire. She tried to remember if he had said anything, the night before, about intending to go out, but at first she could only recall the images of the party. She remembered Agnes sobbing, and the men deciding to search the island. Then it all came back to her. She had walked back with Maggie and the boys, and she had gone to bed alone. She went into the bedroom. There was no sign of Jim's suit or his smart shoes. He had not been home. For a moment the image of Jim taking Elspeth in his arms to dance returned, and there was a sickening moment of suspicion. Then she told herself that she was being foolish and that there must be some other explanation for his absence.

She heard the noise of the generator. It must be ten o'clock. Maggie had told her that they had the generator on for two hours every morning for the freezers and so that the women could use vacuum cleaners and washing machines. Sarah boiled a kettle to make a cup of instant coffee. She used the rest of the hot water for washing, then dressed.

She went outside. There was a cold wind from the north. She walked across the patched tarmac lane to Buness where Alec and Maggie lived. The boys were playing outside with a go-cart. It was Saturday. Parties on Kinness were always held on Friday nights. If they were held on Saturdays, they would have to stop at midnight. Dancing wasn't allowed on a Sunday. She knocked on the front door of the white house. No one answered and she went round to the back. The back door was open and Maggie was in the kitchen pushing children's clothes into a spin dryer.

"Hello," Sarah said. "I was wondering if you knew where Jim was. Did they find Mary?"

She felt young and shy in front of this competent woman engrossed with her domesticity.

Maggie looked up.

"They hadn't done last night, when I went to bed. Alec and Jim came here later, not long after we came back. They came to get some warmer clothes. Jim said that he hadn't unpacked, and borrowed Alec's. They'd looked in all the obvious places then, but she hadn't been found."

"You haven't heard anything this morning?"

Maggie shook her head. "But then I'd be the last person to hear. You'll get used to that."

She straightened her back and switched off the machine.

"I'm going to make a cup of tea," she said. "Come on in and have one."

Sarah hesitated.

"I was going to find Jim. I thought I might be able to help."

"They'll let you know if you can be any use. Come on in."

Awkwardly Sarah went.

Robert found Mary and he wasn't really looking for her. After looking in the empty buildings and Mary's usual hiding places, the men had stopped at Sandwick. Robert had followed them at first, after the dancing had finished, limping after them, afraid of missing anything. But he wasn't invited back to Sandwick and he went home and slept.

He woke early and went looking for wood. Wood was precious on Kinness, and had been more so when he was a boy and imports were unheard of. All the furniture on the island had been made of driftwood. Robert still hoarded driftwood. He did not use it so much himself now, but it pleased him when one of the younger men came begging for a plank to mend a fence or build a new gate.

He scrambled down a rabbit track, sliding on his bottom with his stiff leg out before him, to the rock and shingle at the base of the cliffs, and began to walk along the tide line. His dog was with him as it always was. The fresh wind of the day before promised well. He found some small pieces of wood and began to make a pile above the tide line. He would mark the pile with his own sign—a circle of pebbles—so that anyone else scavenging would know that it was his. He would take it home later, a little at a time.

He found the girl below Ellie's Head, crushed like a doll on the rocks. She had landed above the line of the tide, and her clothes were hardly wet. He felt a moment of pity, but accidental death was not so unusual there. He went back to Sandwick to tell Agnes and Sandy, but before he did so he marked his pile of driftwood with a circle of pebbles.

They asked George to go with them when they went to fetch the body. There had been other accidents around the island—a climber had fallen once from the cliff and someone had drowned after falling from a fishing yawl—and they knew that it meant official questions. If George went with them, he could answer the questions. He was an Englishman and had been a civil servant. He would know how to handle them. George took his camera and insisted on photographing the body before they moved it. They stood awkwardly while he did that, as if embarrassed by his lack of propriety, then lifted her on to a makeshift wooden sledge and pulled her along the shingle and up the rabbit track. He made a note in a small book of the clothes she was wearing. She was wearing the party dress of the night before, and a warm jacket, but not the silk scarf.

He was surprised at how calmly they took the news of her death. Perhaps they had been preparing themselves for it when they had not found her the night before.

"She must have fallen from Ellie's Head," Sandy said.

"She must have run up there for some game. She probably thought that we'd notice sooner that she was gone and chase after her. Then she must have lost her footing and fallen. I should have noticed that she wasn't there."

He turned to George:

"Do you think that's how it was?"

But George did not answer him directly.

"You mustn't blame yourself," George said. "I actually noticed that she wasn't there. I'd promised to dance with her and I went to find her. I thought that she was hiding somewhere. When did you last see her?"

He spoke to all the men who were struggling to pull the sledge over the sharp rocks: Mary's brothers Alec, Jim, and Will, her uncle James, and her father. They stopped to catch their breath, but they could give him no satisfactory answer. They wanted to get it sorted out with him so that he could act as their intermediary with the officials from Baltasay, but they could not remember.

"I saw her dancing with Robert," James said. "But that was a while before the interval. I don't remember seeing her after that."

The others shook their heads. There had been too many drams, they said. It had all been a terrible muddle. They could not remember. They lifted the wooden stretcher again and began the climb up the steep grassy slope. George saw that Will was crying.

They took Mary home to Sandwick, and at Agnes' insistence they took her into her small bedroom and laid her on the bed.

They sat around the big table in the kitchen and Agnes made them breakfast. It was as if she had wasted all her grief in her hysterics of the night before. Now she was calm, numb, and made breakfast as she always did at this time when the men came in from the croft or from fishing.

"Someone should phone to Baltasay," George said tentatively. "Do you want me . . .?"

"No," Jim said. "It should be one of us. I'll go."

He went into the living room to the telephone. Agnes laid the table, put plates of food in front of them, and the men began to eat. She sat in the straight-backed driftwood chair by the range. Absentmindedly she took up her knitting and strapped the horsehair belt around her waist. Island women always used the belt for knitting. It held one of the needles firm. The other began to move quickly as mindlessly she counted stitches and changed coloured wools.

Jim came back into the kitchen.

"It's all sorted," he said. "Because of the way she died there'll have to be formalities. They'll be coming in on the plane, this afternoon."

"Who will?" Alec asked.

"The police. It's routine, they said. They'll be taking the body away with them."

Agnes looked up sharply.

"No," she said. "She's to stay here. She's to be buried here."

"She can be. They said that we could make our own arrangements for the funeral, once the . . . formalities are over."

They were still sitting around the breakfast table when Sarah knocked at the door. Maggie had been friendly. They had drunk tea and talked about the children, Sarah's honeymoon, general plans for the future.

"Do you think that you'll like it here?" Maggie asked at the end, just as Sarah was preparing to go.

"Of course I will. It's Jim's home."

"But you. Will you like it?"

Sarah hesitated. Yesterday she would have been certain, she would have answered immediately: "Of course. Of course I'll like it."

But today she hesitated.

"It'll take some getting used to," she said. "But I want to make a go of it. I'm quite determined."

As she walked up the road to Sandwick the wind blew against her, and she was hot and breathless when she reached the gate. It was an ugly house, big by Kinness standards, square and functional. The yard was ankle deep in mud and two mongrels barked at her as she approached the door. The effort of the walk, the remnant of the hangover and the dogs' muddy footprints on her coat made her angry. It seemed inexcusable to her that Jim had left her alone on her first morning on the island.

The men sitting at the dining table heard the knock on the door but they continued drinking tea and it was Agnes who opened it. Sarah saw that she had been crying, and the anger disappeared. She did not know what to say.

"Come in," Agnes said. "You'll be wondering what happened to Jim. I'm so sorry."

She led Sarah into the room, where the men were still sitting.

"I didn't want to intrude," Sarah said. "Is there any news?"

When she had first seen Agnes, she thought that there must have been a terrible accident, but now, seeing the men carmly at the table, the debris of the breakfast, she thought that she must have been mistaken.

"She's dead," Jim said. "She fell from Ellie's Head. She must have slipped."

Sarah began to cry. She wished that she was alone in the room, and they would all stop staring at her. Agnes took her into her arms as if she were the child.

"That's right," she said. "You cry. It's good to have someone shed some tears for her."

Robert went straight from Sandwick to the post office, the untidy brown dog still at his heels. In the post office Kenneth Dance was serving an old woman. Robert was glad that there were enough people there to give him an audience.

"Mary Stennet's dead," he announced as soon as he got in through the door. There was a satisfying response from the old woman, but Kenneth Dance was harder to rouse to interest. He had left the island when he was a teenager, after telling everyone that he was off south to make his fortune. He had been a postman in Glasgow. Occasionally a touch of Glaswegian still appeared in his speech. He had returned to Kinness when Annie, a distant cousin, had inherited the post office. They had married soon after. He still liked to pretend that he was sophisticated, worldly, wise. He looked up from the postal order he was stamping, but he said nothing.

Robert looked at the daughter, hoping for more reaction from her. Her face was white, but her eyes were blank as if she were remembering something painful, and she, too, was silent.

"She was lying at the bottom of Ellie's Head," Robert said, exacting as much drama as he could from the situation. "I found her. She will have fallen."

"From Ellie's Head?" The daughter looked up sharply, then she said: "The poor child. How horrible."

Robert thought that she was a strange girl, and wondered what had really brought her back to the island. Kenneth and Annie said that she had left her husband, but Robert thought it more likely that he had left her. She would be a difficult woman to live with.

"Do you know what they're doing with the body? I suppose that they'll telephone the police."

Dance was mourning the introduction of the new automatic telephone system. Just a few years ago he would have known the direction of all the calls.

Robert did not have the opportunity to answer. Annie appeared in the shadow of the door which led from the post office into their kitchen.

"Did you say that the child has been found?" she asked.

Elspeth did not give Robert the chance to tell his story. "At the bottom of Ellie's Head," she said quickly, and again he thought how strange she was. "Isn't it a coincidence? At this time of the year. You don't think she meant . . ."

"No," said her mother firmly. "It will have been an accident. Poor Agnes. I will go to Sandwick later and see if there's anything I can do. She was so fond of the girl."

She disappeared back in to the shadow and into the kitchen.

Reluctantly Robert left the post office. He stood for a moment out in the road, not quite sure what he should do next. He would have liked to go to watch the Stennet men fetch the body up the cliff but he did not think that they would like it. A sudden gust of wind caught his cap and blew it from his head. He limped after it, swearing. She's right, he thought. It was this time of year. And it was a day like this. He could not remember exactly how many years ago it was. Sixty maybe. Perhaps more than that. He had only been a boy. That started with a gusty little wind from the north, then in the afternoon it started to blow.

He decided that he did not want to watch the men on Ellie's Head. He was an old man now. He would go and sit in front of his fire, and later perhaps he would have a dram.

In the afternoon the wind increased, so that there were doubts about whether the plane from Baltasay, chartered by the police, would be able to get in. After Sarah's arrival at Sandwick, George Palmer-Jones returned to the school house. He walked up the island against the blustery north wind, and enjoyed the vigorous mindless movement. Jim had asked him if he would come up to the airstrip to meet the police, but he had refused.

"It won't be a pleasant walk in this weather," he had said, "and I don't want to put Alec to any trouble by asking for a lift. I'll be in the school house if they want to see me."

After the first exhilaration of walking, he began to think again about the accident. He tried to reconstruct it so that all the details would be clear in his mind and he would be able to communicate to the police precisely what had happened. When he started, he was quite sure that it was an accident. Mary must have run out of the hall sometime before the interval. He remembered her, as he had seen her the day before, running up the island with pigtails flying behind her. He supposed that some game of her own took her up to Ellie's Head, or perhaps it was a desire to frighten the adults and draw attention to herself.

But what about the secret? he wondered. She was so eager to tell him her secret. It was not like her to forget a thing like that, but she was so unpredictable that perhaps her new game was more important to her. So, she was on Ellie's Head and she must have slipped. He tried to guess how she must have fallen. It was a clear night and there was a moon. He had seen her before clambering about the rocks and down the steep gulleys or "geos" as the local people called them. She was as surefooted as a feral cat. Her deafness seemed not to have affected her sense of balance, and she knew every inch of the place. So how did she fall? Perhaps she had been drinking from the Cup, he thought. That would impair anyone's judgement. If the police thought that it was necessary, they would order a post mortem and that would show whether she had been drinking. In the meantime Jim would know. But where was the green silk scarf? It had been tied tightly round her neck all day. He knew that it had not been left in the hall because he had asked, and it had not been near Mary on the rocks where she fell. He considered the problem all the way back to the school house, but he could think of no satisfactory explanation for the scarfs disappearance. Well then, he thought, perhaps she's been murdered. He did not take this conclusion seriously—it was simply an absurd extension of his argument—but the idea was lodged in his mind and began to bother him.

Despite the weather the plane did land. The two policemen, when they climbed out of the small eight-seater aircraft, were shaking, ill. The pilot was English and it seemed at first that he treated the difficult landing into the gusting wind as a game. Throughout the manoeuvre he shouted flippancies to the terrified men behind him. Later, when they were safely back on Baltasay, he was to say to them:

"Sorry about that, but I had to have a go, you see. One needs to practise in difficult conditions. It might have been a hospital flight, a matter of life and death."

Alec met them in his car, a battered Escort eaten away by rust. It had no road tax, but the policemen did not notice. They were pleasant, sympathetic men, frightened of intruding on recent grief, and after they had talked together with gentle, northern voices, Agnes did not mind entrusting the body of her daughter to them.

The policemen called to see George on their way back to the airstrip. They were in a hurry because the light was falling and it was still windy. The last thing that they wanted was to stay overnight on Kinness.

George explained in detail the circumstances surrounding Mary's disappearance, the search for her, the discovery of the body. The policemen congratulated him on his attention to detail.

"It all seems very straightforward then," one of them said. "An unfortunate accident."

"There is one thing," George said. "She was wearing a scarf at the dance. A silk scarf. It wasn't on her when she died."

"I expect it came off when she fell." The younger man was looking at his watch. He was wondering if he could be home for his son's bedtime. He liked to be back to read the boy a bedtime story. "Then the tide will have taken it."

"It was tied with a knot round her neck. Quite tightly."

"She must have taken it off then at some time before she fell. There's not another explanation."

There is, George thought, but you're too young, and too trusting and too innocent to consider it. But he said nothing and let them rush off to their plane.

When the police had gone, George sat alone in the living room. Jonathan Drysdale had gone out to walk to the north end of the island, to a pool where there were sometimes wild swans. He was planning a trip to catch them and ring them, and he wanted to check that they were there before making the arrangements. He had gone out straight after lunch. Sylvia was in the school room. She was working on some of the craft work she had done with the children. So George could sit there, in the gloom in front of a dying fire, and go through every detail of the thing again, and still it seemed unlikely to him that Mary would have left the hall without telling him about her secret and claiming her dance, and still he could find no explanation for the disappearance of the scarf. So that the thought which had come to him as a ridiculous result of

48

abstract thinking, of isolated reasoning, that the girl might have been murdered, grew more solid. It can't be true, he thought. I'm a meddling old man. But he would not allow himself to escape the facts.

Then Sylvia came in and switched on the light, and threw a couple of logs on to the fire.

"You were asleep," Sylvia said. "You were late last night, and then they got you out so early this morning."

"No," he said. "Not asleep. I was just thinking."

"About Mary?"

He nodded.

"She used to come to see me sometimes," she said. "You know that her parents had asked special permission for her to stay on at school here, because of her handicap. Otherwise she would have started at the big school on Baltasay this term. Sometimes she said that she wished that they would let her go and that it would be fun to live in the hostel with all the others, and at other times she was desperate to stay. I don't know which would have been best for her.. . .

"She used to love to read my magazines, especially the fashion articles. Once I caught her in my bedroom, putting on the make-up which was lying around on the dressing table. I suppose that she was just a normal twelve-year-old and she never had a chance to do that sort of thing at home. Agnes must have been forty when she had Mary so there was quite a generation gap between them. She still treated her as a very young child, and Mary reacted accordingly—tantrums and all."

George had an idea.

"That scarf that she was wearing all day yesterday," he said. "Do you know where she got it?"

"Oh yes," Sylvia said. "It was mine. I gave it to her."

Sarah stayed with Jim at Sandwick in the afternoon while they prepared to receive the police. Alec was there, too, until eventually he went home to tell Maggie what was happening and to collect his car. Will was out all afternoon. No one knew where he had gone.

"I'd better go home," she said when they heard the plane coming low over the house. "They won't want to talk to me."

"No, I don't suppose that they will."

"You'll come back as soon as you can?"

Agnes kissed her before she went and thanked her for being there, and sent her quickly home. She saw Will, standing on the boulder beach below Unsta throwing pebbles into the tide. She almost approached him to offer him comfort, but he seemed absorbed in himself. Perhaps he wanted to be alone, and besides it was very cold.

It was cold in the house too, although there was light. She found paper, sticks and coal in a cupboard in the scullery, but when she tried to light the range it hissed and went out. She had never tried to light a fire before. She felt helpless and incompetent. She had wanted the house to be warm and welcoming for Jim when he came in. She needed to prove to herself that she was a better wife than Elspeth would have been. She wondered if Will was still out on the beach, but when she went outside to call him to help her, he was gone.

When Jim came in the table was laid and the food was ready, but the house was still cold. He showed her how to light the range, but it seemed to her that he was distant and preoccupied.

"I'm so sorry about Mary," she said.

As a nurse she had comforted grieving relatives, but that had been easier. They had been comforted by the uniform, the image of calm authority. She had not needed to think what to say. Now it was an effort, because she was thinking of Elspeth, wondering if he was thinking about her too. He turned the conversation to other matters, to the croft, the house, and neither Elspeth nor Mary was mentioned.

Chapter Five

In the morning they had an argument about going to church.

"But you don't believe in it," Jim said. "You said that it was all superstition. You never went at home. We should start as we mean to go on. If we go today, they'll expect us to go every Sunday."

"It's different here. Perhaps we should go every Sunday."

"Why? Why should we go?"

"It's the custom. Everyone goes. I don't want to upset things. I want to belong."

"This is our home. It's not a bloody museum. We'll never be happy here if we start off by pretending."

"But we should go today. Your mother is so upset. It would hurt her, wouldn't it, if we didn't turn up?"

So he agreed that they would go today. They were standing in the kitchen. The wind had blown itself out. Jim had been out and he held a mug of tea to warm his hands. Sarah was proud because she had managed to light the range. She was wearing jeans and one of Jim's rugby shirts.

"Where have you been?" she asked.

"To watch the milking at Buness. It's all new since I was last here. They did it by hand before. Then I walked around our land. Just to get an idea of what needs to be done. I didn't get a chance yesterday. It's been left to run down. The fencing's in a dreadful state."

"I'll help you," she said. "You'll have to tell me what to do, but I'd enjoy it. We can start this afternoon."

"Not this afternoon," he said. "Not on a Sunday."

"So you do care what they think."

She thought at first that he was angry, but he laughed and caught her round the waist.

"Do you want breakfast?" she asked.

"No. I had some at Buness."

They went into the bedroom to change for church. He put on his wedding suit. She was looking for a respectable dress when she stepped on something and bent down to pick it up. It was the pin caught in the square of paper which had been attached to her wedding dress. She looked again at the words. "He should have been mine." Now they had some meaning. She was quite convinced that the message had been written by Elspeth.

Jim's back was turned to her. He was facing the mirror, knotting his tie. She quickly screwed the paper into a ball, took it into the kitchen, and threw it on to the fire.

As they walked to the kirk the sun came out and lit up the water in the bay. The kirk was just beyond the hall, built of the same stone, with a steeply sloping roof and a bell above it in a small open turret. The bell was ringing a single, monotonous note. They walked past the hall and nearby, just in a field and surrounded by a drystone wall, was a graveyard. Sarah remembered the night of the dance, sitting by a gravestone, thinking that everyone else was in the hall and hearing the running footsteps.

Jim's uncle James was the preacher. Sarah had expected primitive religion, Old Testament Christianity, a rigid formality, but there was nothing of that. James spoke sadly and gently about Mary, about the difficulty of maintaining faith in the face of such tragedy. He gave no easy answers. Then the school choir sang a modern children's hymn accompanied by guitars and recorders. She found it disconcerting. Had she wanted the island to remain a museum, as Jim had said, old-fashioned and predictable, to satisfy her sense of the dramatic? It might perhaps have been easier.

Melissa sat at the back of the church. She had arrived late so that she need talk to no one, but she would have to see Agnes before she and James returned to Kell. Agnes had lost a child now. They had something in common again. As she listened to the children singing she began to weep, and she wondered if the sound of the sweet, high voices was having the same effect on Agnes.

When the service was over, the worshippers stayed in their seats until James had walked down the kirk to the door so that he could greet them as they left.

On the other side of the aisle from the Stennets, Kenneth Dance was talking to his daughter. She sat still and upright with her son close by her side.

"I see that they haven't come from the school house today. You'd think that they'd make the effort this once."

But she was not listening. She was watching Jim Stennet take the hand of his pretty young wife and hold it discreetly under the shelf meant for hymn books and gloves.

"Father," she said suddenly. "It's all been a mistake. I can't stay."

"You don't want to go back to see Gordon?" he whispered. He was horrified.

"No. Not that. But I can't stay on the island."

Annie had heard her. "You've nothing to go back to. Not now. You must stay."

Robert was wondering if someone might invite him back to dinner. Agnes and Sandy did sometimes, but he supposed that the family would be there today. As soon as the service was over and James had opened the door, he loped up the aisle to be there first, and stood there, in the sunshine, with a vacant, begging leer. They all knew what he was doing, but no one took pity on him.

Melissa did not have to find the courage to approach Agnes, because Agnes came to her. Melissa was still sitting in the pew at the back of the church, and Agnes broke way from the rest of the family and sat beside her.

"It was good of you to come," Agnes said.

"I had to come today."

"Mary would have liked the service. She couldn't join in but she liked to watch the children singing. James spoke well. He's a great comfort."

Melissa did not want Agnes to be too comfortable.

"I have to go now," she said. "James will be waiting."

"You won't come back for dinner?"

"No." She could feel the old panic. She had to be out of the church. She had made the effort, and now she had to be away. She stood up.

"Oh well," Agnes said. "Another time, then."

Melissa hurried outside and waited for her husband at a distance from the others so that she would not have to speak to them.

Outside they stood, talking together in the sunshine, the Stennets and the Dances, but when they started walking away down the hill to the houses, they split into separate family groups and each went their own way.

At Sandwick Sarah felt in the way. Maggie was helping Agnes in the kitchen and her own offer of help was refused. The men were talking about sheep. It seemed impossible to her that they could talk about sheep after such a tragedy. In the end she went outside and played with Maggie and Alec's children, until they were all called in for lunch. Then she felt childish and irresponsible.

Over the meal Maggie tried to organize the domestic affairs at Unsta.

"We've put some of our meat in your freezer, but you'll need to order more from the butcher in Baltasay, until your beasts go for slaughter in the spring. You'll have to buy groceries through the shop here—Kenneth Dance has some arrangement with the wholesaler over there, some fiddle, and they won't sell directly to individuals."

Sarah listened to the lecture, tried to be interested. Nobody mentioned Mary. It was as if she had never existed.

They all sat crowded round a table which was not big enough, in a room too small and hot. The men piled their plates with food. After the meal Sarah was allowed to help with the washing up. She watched Agnes absentmindedly blowing her nose on a tea towel and felt that she had seen enough of Jim's family.

She had expected it to be different. The short space of time on Kinness had been as crowded with events as the Sandwick kitchen was with people. She needed to be on her own for a while.

"I think I'll go for a walk," she said, "while it's still light."

"Shall I come with you?" Jim was looking at plans with Alec. He would not have minded going, but he was interested in Alec's ideas and he was pleased when she said she would go alone.

When she left the house she hesitated, uncertain of which way to go. She was used to signposted footpaths on her walks, and was frightened of damaging crops or offending people's privacy. She was beginning to find her bearings on the island, but decided to follow the road north towards the harbour where they had landed the day before. In such a strange place it was reassuring to take a road she already knew. She walked quickly and quite soon passed the school house. Then the island became wilder, less cultivated. On one side of the road was the hill, bare but for heather and sheep, and to the east a low marsh crossd with ditches. There, just by the side of the road was a derelict croft, roofless, much of its walls pulled down, the stone used for building the dyke which marked the beginning of the Kell land. Kell was built into the hill, windswept and exposed to north-easterly winds, sheltered only to the west. The fields around the house were small, surrounded by high walls. It stood well away from the road beyond a small lochan. On the other side of the water she could see James. He was leaning against a gate, smoking a pipe. He had changed out of his suit. He waved and shouted hello, but he did not ask her in.

She walked on as far as the harbour and sat there for a moment on the sandy beach. North of the harbour the road petered into a track which led to the airstrip and eventually to the lighthouse. It rose steeply through bare, windswept grassland and seemed uninviting, rather daunting. She told herself she must have something to explore later, and retraced her steps. Just north of the school house the road forked. She knew that it joined again near Buness. The track which she knew went to the west past Sandwick. She took the easterly road. It, too, followed the fertile area of the island. There were small fields of oats, grass, and vegetables. There was a steep incline and then in a small valley, right next to the road, end on to it, a low grey house. It had a red post box in the wall and a small sign which said: Kinness Post Office and General Stores.

There was no display window. A small boy, Ben, was kicking a football against the wall with intense concentration.

"Hello!" she said. She liked children.

He stared at her but said nothing, then scuttled indoors like a frightened animal.

As she drew level with the kirk the sun was beginning to set below the west cliffs. From every point on the island there was a sight of the sea. She walked off the road and up the hill to the church to get a better view. The pink light of the sun caught the gravestones in the small cemetery, and threw long shadows, so that they could have been prehistoric standing stones. She went over to them and began to read the inscriptions on them. Nearly all of them remembered Stennets, Dances, or Andersons. With pleasure she read the old names—Jacobina, Jerome, Alexander, which recurred generation after generation. Then she saw a name which she recognized and she stopped the idle movement from one stone to another, without reading them carefully. The stone was in a corner, near the protecting wall, and seemed not to have weathered like the others. "Elspeth Dance 1900—1925," it said. Then underneath: "We remember her as she was once and forgive her. The shame is with us all. He should have been hers."

The last phrase was familiar to Sarah. Elspeth must be about twenty-five now, she thought. What can have happened to the poor woman sixty years ago?

Before she could think clearly why she felt that she had seen the last phrase recently, she heard someone coming up behind her and she turned round, startled.

For George Palmer-Jones it had been an unsatisfactory day. He had not slept well. In his mind he had repeated the details of Mary's death, looking for some other fact which might explain it differently. He had found none. And the problem—the need to come to a decision about his future—had not been replaced by the new one. As he tried to sleep the two subjects became linked in his mind, as if the discovery of a logical explanation of the child's death was a test of competence, and if he failed at that, the new venture of his own business would be a failure. If I knew her secret, he thought. If only I knew her secret.

Then there had been the dilemma of whether or not to go to church. It was not that he had no faith. He was church warden in his parish church and he had a strong, though idiosyncratic, commitment. It was a matter of delicacy. He was not sure that he would be welcome. Jonathan and Sylvia never attended services. He knew that when they first came to Kinness they were under considerable pressure to go. Jonathan had even been expected to preach. They had seen it as a matter of principle, and never went, even when the children from school were performing.

Sylvia did not appear for breakfast. The two men sat at the pine table in the small, immaculate kitchen, drank percolated coffee from expensive hand-thrown mugs. George felt a deep nostalgia for the large untidy kitchen at home, for tea from a jumble-sale teapot, and for Molly.

"I'm sorry that Molly couldn't come this year," he said.

"So am I. Sylvia misses the company."

"She did want to come, but there was a crisis in the refuge for battered wives where our daughter works. One of her staff is sick. Molly said she'd help for a while. I'm not sure that she's settled to retirement."

Nor have I, he thought. He said:

"I thought I might go to church this morning."

Jonathan was disappointed, offended. "I was planning a walk," he said, "see if the wind brought in anything interesting."

"I'll come with you then." It was easier that way. He was the Drysdales' guest. He supposed that Jonathan enjoyed his company on these walks around the island. It was hard to tell. The previous visits to Kinness had been different. Molly mixed with everyone. She had made them all laugh. There had been a sense that they were on holiday. It occurred to him that he was there under false pretences—he had only been invited in the past because of Molly's ability to make them happy. The least he could do was to go birdwatching with his host. He must be unsettled, he thought. He never usually needed an excuse to go birdwatcbing.

It was a depressing walk. There were no birds.

"It's like this sometimes," Jonathan said, "then the wind goes south-east and something unusual turns up. Of course I miss a lot."

"It must be difficult to get an accurate record when you're on your own here."

"Impossible. I've tried to get Sylvia involved, but she doesn't seem interested. Then the big falls of birds always seem to happen during the week while I'm at school."

"When does term start again?"

"It's already started. The older ones were supposed to go out on the boat two weeks ago, but they were allowed to stay on becaue of the party. The crew are doing a special run to Baltasay tomorrow to take Will Stennet and the others out. That will make covering the island more difficult, too. Will is quite keen on natural history. He's more of a botanist than an ornithologist but he knows all the regular migrants and he's improving all the time. He helped a lot with seabird ringing earlier this season. He's very handy to have on the cliffs—an excellent climber."

They were back at the school house in time for lunch. Sylvia was spreading a floral print cloth over the dining-room table. The house smelled of English Sundays. She was wearing a soft white wool dress. She had done her hair differently—it was piled on to her head and fastened with combs—and she was wearing make-up. She offered them sherry.

"This is very civilized," George said.

"We don't entertain very often. I like to make the most of it when we do. It isn't worth making the effort for Jon. He only cares about auks."

"What did you say?" Jonathan had gone straight to his bookshelf and had taken down a copy of *Birds of the Western Palearctic*. He and George had been discussing snowy owls and there was something he wanted to check. He had not been listening to his wife.

Sylvia laughed, went over to her husband, and kissed him lightly on the forehead.

"You see? He's incorrigible. What can I do with him?"

The food was good and Palmer-Jones enjoyed talking about birds with Jonathan and the island with Sylvia. She could capture the individuals of Kinness with one witty phrase—cruel, but amusing. After the meal they sat by the fire, drank coffee, and read. It was very peaceful. I'm an old man, George thought. This is how I should be spending my time. After all, it's not my problem. But he could not leave it alone. There were two questions—had Mary been murdered? And if so, what should he do about it?

He got up from his seat by the fire and went to stand by the window. He looked towards Kell and the steep, grey hill beyond. Someone was walking past the deserted croft by Kell. It was Jim Stennet's new wife. She was lost to his view beyond the post office. She stopped and looked about her, then hurried on.

"I think I'll go for a walk," he said. "Get some fresh air and walk off some of that delicious lunch."

Sylvia looked up from her book and smiled. He was afraid for a moment that she was going to offer to accompany him, but she only nodded. Jonathan was still absorbed and seemed not to hear him.

He found Sarah in the graveyard. She was studying one of the gravestones and seemed engrossed in the inscription. She turned suddenly and he realized that he had startled her.

"Excuse me," he said.

"That's all right. I'm just enjoying the last of the sun." She felt foolish, standing in the graveyard.

"And the peace. I'm sorry to disturb you."

Suddenly she was pleased to see him. He seemed very English and ordinary. Very familiar.

"I think perhaps we should walk on down to the road past the school house," he said. "I came to find you. I need your help."

"But I've told you. I don't know anything about birds. I shouldn't be any help."

"It's not that. I need your advice." He hesitated. "It's about Mary."

"I don't understand. I thought that it was all decided. The police accepted that you were an independent witness. They seemed quite satisfied about how she fell, and that no one could have prevented it."

"That's just my problem. They *are* quite satisfied. But I'm not."

He hesitated again. "I don't believe that her death was an accident. I think that she must have been pushed."

"You think that she was murdered?" Her voice was incredulous and the word sounded ridiculous.

"Perhaps I should explain why. I saw Mary on Friday morning just after we had landed. She was very excited about the party and she said she had a secret to share with me. At the party she mentioned it again, and I promised to dance with her later. She was enjoying herself and there was something she was keen to tell me. I don't believe that she would have run away from that.

"Then there was the scarf. Did you notice that she was wearing it all day? Sylvia Drysdale had given it to her and she was very proud of it. But when we found the body she wasn't wearing it. She fell above the tide line, so it wouldn't have been washed away. I had a look for it yesterday at the top of Ellie's Head and around the hall, but I haven't found it. If it was taken from her either before or after she fell, it means that someone else was implicated in her death."

He turned to her.

"Did you notice whether she had anything alcoholic to drink at the dance?"

She considered carefully.

"I don't remember very well," she said. "I'd had quite a lot to drink myself. But I don't think that she can have done. We didn't allow the children to get at the Cup, and they all had orange squash for the toasts."

"So how did she come to fall? There was a moon on Friday night. I've seen her climbing around the cliffs like the other children after gulls' eggs and she was more surefooted than any of them."

She was not at all convinced.

"I don't believe it," she said. "Those all seem such little things. They can't mean that someone murdered her. It seems melodramatic, silly."

"I can't change facts," he said quietly. "I have tried to find a different way of explaining them, but I haven't succeeded yet. There may be another explanation. I came to talk to you to ask if you think I should try to find it."

"What do you mean?"

"The police are satisfied that Mary died accidentally. Perhaps I should leave it at that."

"But if you believe that she was murdered, you must do something about it."

"I'm not sure," he said. "This is a special place, precarious. If I meddle I might endanger its survival."

"But it's not a museum," she said, repeating the phrase yet again. "I'm not at all sure that you're right about Mary's death, but just because someone's been born on Kinness or is married to someone who was born here, they're not above the law. Surely the same moral code applies here as anywhere else."

She knew that she sounded pompous, and realized in a moment of insight that she was trying to convince herself. She had wanted Kinness to be like a museum, dramatically different from anywhere else. That had been the attraction. Now she was here, she had to think again. She did not want to be a church-going, submissive, housewifely museum exhibit. She felt very confused.

"If you believe that Mary was murdered," she persisted, "you must do something about it."

"But what? I did try to explain my doubts to the police, but they were as sceptical as you are."

"What would you do if you were on the mainland?"

"I'd talk to everyone, ask a lot of questions, understand what had happened myself, until I had sufficient evidence to take to the police."

"You seem used to this sort of thing."

"Yes. Before I retired I worked for the Home Office. I worked very closely with the police."

"You must do the same thing thing here," she said. "Ask your questions. Get to the bottom of it."

They were both silent for a moment. The sun had nearly

61

disappeared. The island seemed very calm and very beautiful, caught in the orange light.

"Perhaps you're right," he said. "I shall have to think it through for myself, be certain in my own mind first. I know that I've not convinced you, but if I decide to go ahead, will you help me?"

"I have to, don't I?" she said. "I can't give that sort of advice if I'm not prepared to follow it myself."

"Do you know of anyone who would benefit from Mary's death?"

"No."

"I've been thinking about opportunity. Who could have left the hall without being noticed? It wouldn't have taken very long to follow her up to Ellie's Head, push her off, and run back."

"To fit in with your facts the murderer must have arranged to meet her there. He or she must have given her a good reason for leaving the party."

"Yes."

She shook her head.

"It could have been anyone," she said. "Especially in the interval when the band stopped playing. People were coming and going all the time. I came out for a breath of fresh air and no one seemed to notice that I'd gone missing."

She stopped suddenly.

"I heard footsteps while I was outside," she said. "Running footsteps."

"Did you? You don't know what time that was?"

"No."

She put her hands in her jacket pockets. "It's getting cold," she said. "I'd better go back to Sandwick, find Jim."

The church bell began to ring for the evening service.

George Palmer-Jones walked with her and stopped at the gate by Sandwick.

"Don't put yourself in an awkward position with the family," he said. "There'd have to be a compromise anyway, whoever you married and wherever you lived. This is a special place and I don't want to spoil it for you."

"You won't," she said. Despite her Sunday-best dress she climbed the gate and ran through the mud to the house. She seemed almost excited.

Sylvia and Jonathan were still in the same positions by the fire. George felt brisk and energetic coming in from the cold, and he had an urge to rouse them from their lethargy. He had told Sarah that he would find out what had happened to the child by asking questions. He could start now.

"Did you have a pleasant walk?" Sylvia asked lazily. She stretched and George thought that she looked like a big, voluptuous chestnut cat.

"Yes thank you."

"I'll go and make some tea."

"No," he said. "Not yet if you don't mind."

She seemed surprised but curled back into her chair.

"When did you give the green scarf to Mary?"

"On Friday afternoon. School finished early so that the children could go to welcome Jim and Sarah, and she came in immediately afterwards. Jonathan was still in the classroom. She had admired it several times and she wanted something pretty to wear to impress her new sister-in-law. It wasn't expensive—not real silk—so I gave it to her. Is it important?"

"I think so. I think that her death may not have been an accident."

"What do you mean?"

"I think that she may have been pushed." He realized that he had avoided the word "murdered."

"Oh George, are you sure? It doesn't seem very likely. The people here are far too boring to do anything like that."

She could not take him seriously. She was laughing at him, accusing him of senility, of an obsession with crime. He did not answer her. Jonathan looked up, at last, from his book.

"*Are* you sure, George?" he asked.

"No. But I'm not satisfied that it was an accident."

He explained why he could not accept the theory that Mary had slipped over the cliff.

"Yes," Jonathan said. "I see. It does seem strange."

He continued to give George his full attention. His eyes did not stray back to the book on his knee. George went on:

"Mary was going to tell me a secret. I was wondering what it could be. You know all the Kinness scandal, Sylvia. Has anyone got any deadly secrets?"

"We all have secrets," she said brightly, "but I don't think any of them are deadly. Really, George, aren't you imagining it all?"

She put aside her book and stood up. "Now," she said. "I'll make some tea." They heard her in the kitchen, and she came in again soon after with a tray. She put it on a small table but did not sit down. She stood where she was in front of the fire. In the firelight she seemed flushed.

"I thought that I might go out on the boat tomorrow," she said, "and stay on Baltasay for a few days. I could come back on Friday. I need some time away from Kinness. Perhaps I could treat myself, stay in the hotel, do some shopping. I've been feeling rather trapped lately."

She knew that she was saying too much and was abruptly silent. The men watched her. The speech had come as a shock.

"Of course you must go if you feel like that," Jonathan said gently. "We'll manage here."

He turned back to his book. She sat down and began to pour out the tea. The trip to Baltasay was not mentioned again all evening.

Chapter Six

The Ruth Isabella always left Kinness early in the morning. In the summer there were so many hours of daylight that if the boat left at three in the morning, it would have been possible to see. In December she was halfway to Baltasay before it was dawn. It made no difference. The boat always left between seven and seven-thirty. The crew were usually at the harbour by six.

Jim had decided to go out with them. He could say goodbye to Will, and he would be an extra crew member on the way home. Sarah woke when he did and heard him moving carefully about the house.

She got up and dressed. In the kitchen he was making sandwiches by candlelight. He was concentrating hard on what he was doing. He was obviously trying not to make any noise which might wake her. She kissed him, touched by his care.

"I would have done that last night," she said. "I should have realized that you would need something to take with you."

"It's no problem."

"I thought that I'd come down to the harbour with you and see you off. I'd like to see Will again. You don't mind?"

"Of course not. I won't go if you don't want me to. You won't be lonely?"

"No. I'll be glad of a day to get sorted out. I can finish unpacking, start thinking about what needs to be done to the house."

It was true. If he was there she would feel that she should tell him about her conversation with George Palmer-Jones, about her jealousy of Elspeth. A married couple should share things like that. As it was she did not know how to begin to confide in him.

Outside Alec was waiting with the lorry. The air was cold and damp. It was still dark. They climbed into the cab with him. It smelled of diesel and fish.

"Sarah thought that she'd come to see me off," Jim said. He had to shout over the noise of the engine.

Alec grinned. She was squeezed between the two men.

"That's all right," he said. "It's nice to have some pretty company." He put his arm around her. She squirmed away from him. Jim sat stiff and disapproving on the other side.

"Maggie always gets up with me on boat days," Alec said. Perhaps he was trying to prove to her, and to Jim, that he was really harmless, tame. "She has to see to the milking and she says it's a good time to get the baking done, before the boys are awake."

She would, Sarah thought.

Just as they were approaching Sandwick the lorry stalled. Alec could not start it again. He swore. Sandy and Will had been waiting outside Sandwick. Will had a large rucksack and his guitar and seemed out of place standing by the road. He could have been any student, hitching a lift back to college.

"It's no good," Alec said. "This bloody thing is only fit for the scrapyard. I'll go back to Buness to get the car. If you want to start walking, I'll pick you up if I see you."

Just get me out, Will thought. I'd walk all the way to Baltasay to get away from this place.

They climbed down from the cab and stood in the middle of the road looking at the lorry.

"Someone should go to the post office and tell Kenneth Dance that we'll be late collecting the mail," Sandy said, "otherwise he'll make a fuss. You do that, Will. You can leave your stuff here and Alec will collect it." He spoke quietly, but he was in charge. His only daughter had died but he would not allow his grief to give Alec an excuse to take control. "Go on down to the harbour, Jim. Start loading up. There are a lot of gas cylinders. I'll just go in and tell Agnes what's happening. She can telephone to the post office in Baltasay and tell them we'll be a bit late."

"Do you still want to come?" Jim asked Sarah.

"Yes. I can help you load the gas cylinders."

She knew that he was about to say that they would be too heavy for her or that he could do it alone, but he said nothing. He's trying very hard, she thought. She took his arm.

In Kell James was making tea. He was always up early. Although Alec could supply milk for the whole island with his cows and his smart new milking parlour, they still kept a cow at Kell for hand milking. Before, Melissa had looked after the animals on the croft, but now he did it all, even the women's work of milking and egg collecting. He would not have minded if it had made her well. He would have liked to go to watch the boat off. He had been a member of the crew once, but had given it up when Melissa started being so depressed. He had been afraid of leaving her alone all day. He poured tea into a special cup which he kept for her, and took it into the bedroom. He had to light the gas light. Outside there was low cloud over the hill and it was still dark. She woke up when he went in.

"I was having a lovely dream," she said. He was still thinking abut the boat.

"The *Ruth* will be getting ready to go now. The children are going back to Baltasay to school today."

Her face clouded with pain, but cleared again.

"If you see them going past say goodbye to them for me," she said. "I'll get up soon and have breakfast ready for you, when you come back."

She lay back in bed until she heard the front door bang and she knew he was outside.

In the post office Kenneth Dance was angry. If he did not have the mail ready when the lorry stopped outside, Alec Stennet was banging on his door and yelling at him. He had been waiting now for half an hour and there was no sign of the lorry. It would be just like the Stennets to cancel the extra sailing without telling him.

There was a tap at the door. Will stood outside. Dance glared at him.

"Yes?" he said aggressively.

"The lorry's broken down. Alec has gone to fetch his car and he'll collect the mail in that."

"Will he then? Well he can load the sacks himself. I'm back to my bed."

Kenneth Dance shut the door on the boy and went upstairs. He noticed that Elspeth's bedroom door was open, but thought nothing of it. He went into the bedroom, where his wife was still asleep, but he did not undress.

Robert heard the lorry starting, from the two-roomed house where he had lived alone since his mother had died twenty years before. He had never lived anywhere else, had never been on the mainland. Then he heard the lorry stall and listened to the choking splutter as Alec tried to start it again. He was already half dressed, and he pulled on warm outdoor clothes and his heavy black boots. He had to bend his back uncomfortably to lace the boot on his bad leg, but it never occurred to him to wonder what might happen to him when he could no longer bend like that. He wanted to know what had happened to the lorry, and what the Stennet family might do about it. He called to his dog and went outside. He could hear the men talking in the road and the footsteps as they walked away. He was disappointed. Nothing exciting had happened after all. There was nothing to see.

He wondered if he should go to the harbour to watch the *Ruth Isabella* out, but decided that he would not go. It would be different if a fishing boat had put in there for shelter. Then there was talk of having the Hill Dipping Gather and the Lamb Share out soon, and he wanted to get some idea of how many of the lambs would come to him. It was just starting to get light.

Palmer-Jones was surprised to hear movement in the school house early that morning. He had not believed that Sylvia would leave the island. He had thought that her outburst was a dramatic expression of her frustration at being on Kinness, and that talking about it would be enough. Now the soft movement, the hurried whispers between husband and wife, suggested escape, and it seemed important that he should talk to Sylvia before she went.

She must have been on her way out when he heard her, because by the time he had dressed she had left the house. He went outside and a raw dampness made him put up the hood of his jacket. It was still quite dark and the immediate stretch of the road was hidden by a fold in the hill so he could not see her, but he knew that she must have followed the road towards the harbour. He was afraid that the boat would leave before he had the opportunity to speak to her and he started to walk more quickly. The cold air made him feel stiff and breathless, and he thought: when I was young I could have run this. The road turned, so that he should have had a view across the island towards the harbour, but a damp mist seemed to crawl down from the hill and he could see only a block of shadow to separate the hill from the sky. He stopped to listen, but there was no sound of footsteps. I must have missed her, he thought, but he walked on.

When he came to the derelict croft, he thought he heard whispered voices, but decided that it must be the wind in the stone. Taft, the croft was called, and it had been lived in by Dances before the depopulation of the islands began. He did not know that the boat would be late and was afraid that it would go before he could see Sylvia. Then he heard running footsteps behind him on the road. As he turned to see who it was the mist cleared from the hill above and he saw Robert staring down at him. The person running along the road was Sylvia. She seemed untidy, excited.

"Where have you been?" he asked. "You may miss the boat."

"I don't think so," she said. "The lorry hasn't passed yet."

"I left the school house after you. Where have you been?"

She shrugged. "I don't walk as quickly as you. I must have lost my way in the mist."

There was no possibility that this could have been true.

"I heard people talking," he said. "Did you meet anyone?"

"No. Of course not. Who would I meet on a day like this?"

Alec's car came along behind them then. He must have seen them in his headlights. The car stopped and he shouted:

69

"Do you want a lift down?"

Before she could answer George called back: "No thanks. We're nearly there now."

Alec was about to start off again when she said: "Don't leave without me. I want to come to Baltasay."

He nodded and drove away.

George turned to her, took her arm.

"You know Mary's secret, don't you?" he said quietly. "You must tell me, you know."

"I'm sorry," she said. "I really can't believe Mary's death was anything but an accident, and in that case there's nothing to tell."

As they walked down the hill and approached the harbour the mist cleared and the sky grew lighter. George could make out the horizon of the headland beyond the harbour and the *Ruth Isabella* in the water. Alec was pulling a sack of mail from the back of his car. Jim, Sandy, and Will were already aboard. A mother and father were calling goodbye to teenage daughters.

"Why are you leaving Kinness?" he asked abruptly. "What are you frightened of?"

"Nothing," she said. "Why should I be frightened?"

"Don't go," he said. He felt that if only he had time to speak to her he would make her understand and persuade her to talk to him. She was surprised by the request, by the breach of social convention. She smiled.

"Don't worry," she said. "Jonathan's a good cook."

Sandy Stennet shouted to her from the *Ruth Isabella*.

"If you can get aboard, Mrs. Drysdale, we're ready to go."

George watched helplessly as Alec helped her on to the *Ruth Isabella*. Alec climbed on afterwards and the boat began to move away. The sea was smooth and the boat moved slowly, so there almost no wake.

The parents on the quay drifted off, and Sarah and George were left alone. He looked at his watch. It was a quarter past eight.

"The boat was late this morning," George said.

"Yes. The lorry broke down. We all had to walk except Alec. He was furious. There was no one in the post office to help him load up. Apparently there was a lot of knitwear of Annie's to go out, besides the mail. It took him longer than he expected."

"Did the rest of you walk down together?"

"No. Jim and I were together. We got to the harbour first. Will arrived next—he had been over to the post office to tell Kenneth Dance that Alec would be late. Sandy didn't get here until just before Alec. I don't know why he took so long. Perhaps he was hoping for a lift."

"Did anyone leave the quay after you'd got there?"

"What's all this about?"

I hear voices in the mist, he thought. How can I tell her that? She'll think I'm a fool.

"Oh," he said vaguely, "it may be important."

But she humoured him.

"Jim went up the road once to see if Alec was coming. Alec did take much longer than we expected and Jim was afraid that the car might have broken down, too. I'm not sure about Will. He may have wandered off. He seemed very restless and he didn't help much with the boat. Does that help?"

"I don't know. Thank you. Did you see anyone on the road as you walked down?"

She shook her head. They began to walk back to the crofts. When they reached the school house, he asked her in for coffee. He was reluctant to let her go. Then he would be alone with the problem, with notes on Mary's death in his tiny writing in his notebook.

Jonathan was already in the classroom and they were alone in the kitchen, but they did not mention Mary. He thought that perhaps she had reconsidered her offer of help. She did not know what to make of him. He frightened her a little with his politeness, his precise speech, his upright posture. She watched the children run into the playground, then said that she would go. He saw her off sadly. He did not know what to do. He felt powerless to take charge of events. If only there was something conclusive, he thought. If only there was something to prove that Mary had been pushed. If only I had the scarf . . .

In the windswept playground Ben Dance crouched in a corner and drew on the asphalt with a stone. Grandma had given him breakfast today. He wondered where his mother was. Perhaps she had disappeared like Dad and Mary. He had wanted Dad and Mary to disappear, but he would not want to lose his mother. He felt that he might cry, and frowned to stop himself. He had been a very good boy lately, so there was no reason for her to go. He had felt, secretly, that he must have some magic. He had wanted Dad to disappear for as long as he could remember, and then suddenly he had. When they moved to Kinness, Mary had been so bossy and had spoiled all his games, and he had hoped that she would go, too, in the same way. And she had. That must be some sort of magic. But it would be terrible if it happened to his mother. The bell went and he ran inside, and was distracted from his anxieties by Peter and Jane and First Step Maths.

On her way home Sarah called into the post office. She needed groceries, flour, cheese, stamps. Kenneth Dance was alone in there. He sat on a high stool behind the counter.

"Yes?" he said. He was staring at her.

The room was heated by a Calor Gas heater and the smell of the gas and the sudden warmth made her feel slightly faint. She ordered some stamps, but he did not move. He sat behind the counter like a Dickensian clerk at his desk and stared at her over his glasses. She was embarrassed and increasingly uncomfortable in the stuffy room. At last he took his eyes from her face and pushed the stamps over the counter towards her.

She was about to ask for the other goods she needed when the door opened and Elspeth came in. Her long hair was tangled and there was a hole in her tights. She was wearing a moth-eaten fur coat and a shapeless knitted hat. Her father ignored Sarah.

"Where have you been?" he said to Elspeth. "We were worried sick."

"I went out for a walk."

"We thought that perhaps you'd gone out on the *Ruth.*"

"I did think about it. But I would have told you first. I wouldn't leave Ben—you know that."

"He wanted to know where you were."

"Did he go off to school all right?"

Kenneth Dance nodded grudgingly. "He ran off early. You should have been here to see him off."

"Yes," she said. "I should have been."

"Don't do it again. Your mother's been ill with worry."

Sarah watched with interest. It seemed to her that Kenneth Dance was over-reacting. Elspeth Dance turned away towards the kitchen door, then returned to face Sarah.

"How's Jim?" she asked.

"He's well," Sarah said.

"I never meant to hurt him. I hope he understands."

They stood for a moment looking at each other.

"Did you pin a note to my wedding dress?" Sarah said suddenly.

"No." Elspeth's surprise seemed genuine, but Sarah was not convinced. "He should have been mine," the note had read, and "He should have been hers" was the inscription on the gravestone of the original Elspeth Dance. The similarity came to her suddenly and seemed too much of a coincidence.

Elspeth disappeared into the kitchen, then Kenneth Dance served Sarah as if the conversation had never taken place.

In the school Jonathan Drysdale was irritated, as he always was, by the younger children's inability to concentrate. He would never have chosen to specialize in primary teaching elsewhere. Sylvia had been glad to help him with the little ones, and when they had first moved to Kinness they had worked together in the classroom. They had been happy then, he thought. The walls of the school room had been covered by the collages and pictures she had inspired in the infants, and he had taken the older ones for more formal, academic subjects. Then Maggie Stennet had begun the campaign of complaint because her youngest son was slow to learn to read. When the Drysdales had first moved to Kinness they had seen Maggie as an ally. She, after all, had been a teacher. Then twelve months before, her attitude towards them had changed. Sylvia was not qualified to teach, she said. She might have been to art college but she had no degree in education. Stuart could read fluently by the time he was six, so why was Neil still bringing home picture books? Jonathan wanted to reply: "Because he's dim, he takes after your husband," but he had promised more structure for the reception group, promised to spend more time on the basics with them. He had tried, too. He had sat at the double table where they sat, perched on a ridiculous small chair, surrounded by flash cards and Ladybird books, but he could get no response from them, and while he was there the bigger children got bored with the work he had set them, and began to chat and fidget. He had longed at times to be in a large city school with classes streamed according to age and ability. There had been no improvement in the infants' reading skills, and at times of boredom Sylvia had drifted back into the classroom to help. Neil, miraculously, had begun to read, but Maggie continued to complain. Now she said that the Drysdales did not participate fully in island affairs, did not encourage the children to understand their own history. He had recieved a warning letter from the Education department on Baltasay. Maggie had started complaining there.

Jonathan walked to the infants' table and started them copying letters in a print workbook. He set a series of arithmetic problems on the blackboard for the older group, then sat at his desk. He began to think of Sylvia again, but knew that would lead nowhere, so he returned to his favourite subject. He imagined his black guillemot paper, illustrated with immaculate diagrams, the argument followed through with perfect logic, and the credit he would receive when it was published in a respected academic journal.

Sarah returned to Unsta determined to put Elspeth from her mind. Jealousy was ridiculous. Elspeth was obviously a spoilt, neurotic woman and there was no competition between them. She would not mention her conversation with Elspeth to Jim. If he did not want to discuss his former girlfriend, she would respect his privacy. Elspeth was someone to feel sorry for, and pity made her safe.

In this strong, confident mood she began to make plans for the house. She did not want to bully Jim into building yet—that could wait for the spring—but she could make Unsta more civilized. They would need carpet, new units for the kitchen, fresh paint, curtains. She walked through the house from the kitchen to the bedroom, imagining how it would be, irritated because she could not start at once. She could start in the garden, she thought. It had been cultivated until recently but it was full of weeds. She wanted to dig it over before the frost came. She went to Buness and borrowed a spade and fork. She worked all afternoon, and imagined Jim's pleasure when he saw how much she had achieved.

At half past three Maggie called over the wall at her.

"I'm going to collect the children from school, then I'm going on to meet the boat. Will you come?"

Sarah went inside to wash her hands and change her shoes. Maggie was still looking over the wall when she returned.

"You've cleared a good lot there," Maggie said grudgingly, and it seemed to Sarah that she was disappointed.

They were a little early at the school and waited at the gate.

"I suppose that Neil will have been messing with paint and glue with Mrs. Drysdale again," Maggie said. "It's not right. She's not qualified, you see. He should be properly taught. That's what Drysdale's been paid for. If they want an infants' teacher, they should advertise."

Sarah remembered that Maggie had been a teacher. Perhaps she was hoping for a job in the school.

"She won't be there today," Sarah said. "She went on the *Ruth Isabella*."

"Did she then? I wonder how long she'll be away for. They should both leave. For good. Neither of them fits in here."

It occurred to Sarah then that there was a more personal animosity between Maggie and Sylvia. She remembered suddenly how Alec had waltzed with Sylvia at the party, holding her very close, and realized that she recognized a note of jealousy in Maggie's voice.

The school bell rang and the children ran out.

As the *Ruth Isabella* approached the harbour Sarah watched Jim

75

with pride. He seemed so surefooted, so competent. He saw her and smiled. She wished that some outsider was there so that she could have pointed to Jim and said: "That's my man. He belongs here and so do I." She looked around for George Palmer-Jones. He would have done, but he was not there. She assumed that he was embarrassed about his foolish allegation that Mary had been murdered. His silence that morning proved that he had changed his mind. She turned back to the boat and waited for Jim to come ashore.

Ben Dance did not go home immediately after school. He wanted to hurt his mother because she had not been there in the morning to have breakfast with him or to see him off to school. He followed the other children down the road towards the harbour, but on the way he was distracted and played alone until long past teatime.

On Ellie's Head George searched the rocky outcrops and peered down the geos looking for a cheap green scarf. Then he climbed down the rabbit track to the beach below, moving the shingle with his Wellingtons and scouring the rock pools, until it was too dark to see.

Chapter Seven

Sandy Stennet and Kenneth Dance decided together that they would have the Hill Gather. They met, like elder statesmen on neutral territory, by the church early in the morning and looked at the sky, and lifted fingers to the wind. The fine weather would hold, they decided. They would share responsibility for holding the Hill Gather. All summer the hill sheep had been left to wander. Now they had to be collected for dipping, and each family would be allocated their share of the hill lambs. It was a formidable task to round up the sheep. The hill covered an area of nearly two square miles. The men and dogs would stand at the north end of Kinness, near the lighthouse and over the hill in a line, driving the sheep before them. Just north of Kell a stone wall had been built from the road to the west cliffs. The sheep would be driven down that and collected into one of Kell's fields. There they would be dipped and sorted.

Alec had mended the lorry, and collected all the men—Stennets and Dances—and took them to the lighthouse. Sarah was the only woman there. They allowed her to come because she was new, and she had no other responsibilities—no animals at the croft or children, but some of the older men grumbled at her presence. It was felt to be not quite lucky. The lorry stopped by the school house and Alec went to the door and asked George Palmer-Jones if he would like to help. The operation depended on having enough men to cover the hill, and with Will back at school they would be short of people. In previous times the school had been closed for the Hill Gather and they had used the older boys to fill the gaps, but no one approached Jonathan Drysdale to ask for his cooperation. They were certain that he would refuse.

It was a bright, sunny day with a gusty breeze which broke the surface of the pools on the hill, so that the reflected light scattered in all directions. There was white spume from the waves on the sea and the fulmars and kittiwakes seemed to be playing in the wind. Sandy Stennet arranged the men on the hill, meticulously checking with Kenneth Dance that he agreed with the way the men had been placed. He put George Palmer-Jones at the end of the line, nearest the west cliffs. The land was flatter there, and not so boggy. It would be easier walking, with fewer sheep. George knew why he had been placed there and it added to his sense of helplessness. He remembered the ridicule in Sylvia's voice, and being placed at the end of the line, next to old Robert, seemed to him an added insult.

At last Sandy was satisfied and the men began to move. There was a noise of dogs barking and men clapping and whistling to send the sheep forward. Despite his hurt pride at being given the easiest position on the line George began to enjoy himself. There was some warmth in the sun and he had the spectacular view of the cliffs and the sea. He felt close to the sky. Robert's dog was chasing madly between them, doing their work for them. They walked slowly so that the men who had to climb the steep rise of the hill could keep up with them. George could see them still in line, like a row of telegraph poles. The island was wider here, and the whistling and calling became more frantic as sheep escaped behind them. There would be another gather, later in the month, to collect the sheep they had missed.

Then they could see the wall and there seemed to be hundreds of sheep jostling in front of them. The sheep were usually white but there were a good number of more valuable black and brown animals among them. The noise of bleating sheep was added to that of the dogs and the men. As the sheep hit the wall some of them ran west towards George and he ran towards them shouting and waving his arms like the other men.

As he approached the wall he saw someone walking along the cliffs on the other side of it. It was Elspeth Dance. He recognized the tangled curly hair, the fur coat. He recognized, too, the green silk scarf, which she wore around her neck and which the wind caught and blew out like a streamer.

George waited for her at the wall. The sheep were easier to control now. They were already running down the side of the wall, and some had reached the field at Kell. He was no longer needed. When she saw him, she began to turn away as if she wanted to avoid conversation, but he climbed over the wall, proud of his agility in front of her, and he joined her in her walk back along the cliffs.

"You don't mind if I join you," he said, in such a way that she could not refuse. She did not answer and seemed so preoccupied that he wondered if she had heard him.

"Would you mind telling me," he said, "where you found the scarf?"

"Do you know who it belongs to?" she asked. "My son gave it to me. He promised that he hadn't stolen it."

"You don't recognize it?" She shook her head.

"When did he give it to you?"

"Yesterday. He was late home from school. It was a kind of peace offering."

"Did he tell you where he found it?"

"No. He wouldn't say."

"It was Mary's," he said. "She was wearing it at the party. Just before she died."

She seemed bewildered.

"Then why did he have it?"

"I don't know. Would you mind if I asked him? I told the police that I was worried because the scarf hadn't been found. It would tie up all sorts of loose ends if I could clear it up."

"I don't know." She did genuinely seem to want to help. "He's been through a lot lately. I wouldn't want to upset him."

"I would be very gentle. I have a grandson of about his age."

She seemed reassured. "Very well then. He'll be at school now, but if you meet me at the school house at a quarter to four, you can see him then."

He would have been happy to walk down the island with her, but she seemed to want to be on her own.

"Could I keep the scarf?" he said before she went. "I'm sorry, but the police may want it."

"Ben will be sad," she said. "He was so proud to have a present to give me."

She removed the scarf and handed it to him, then said goodbye and walked off, along the path by the cliff.

Sarah was enjoying herself immensely. This was what island life was all about, she thought, a communal effort for the good of the whole island. She walked over the hill beside Jim and felt excited as the sheep approached the wall and were driven into the field. She joined in the cheers as the gate was closed behind them. This is better than working inside, in a hospital ward, she thought, wondering how she could ever have doubted that she would settle on Kinness. But as she walked past Kell with Jim, on her way home to Unsta for lunch, she saw Melissa's sad, frightened face at a dark window and suddenly she was not quite so certain.

Once Elspeth was out of sight of George Palmer-Jones she stopped, and sat on the spongy soil at the top of the cliff where the puffin holes and rabbit burrows seemed only to be held together by the roots of the thrift. She thought of the story of Ellie, her namesake, who had died by jumping over the cliff in 1925. If I were going to commit suicide, she thought, that's how it would be. There must be an exhilaration in the act of jumping, in the speed of the air. It must be like flying. But she knew that it was impossible for her to think of dying. She had Ben to care for and he had lost enough.

She looked at her watch. It was nearly lunchtime and her parents would be worried about her. She should try to do more for them, she thought, help in the shop. She owed them that at least. If she had married Jim, everything would have been different. She remembered the letter she had written to him from Glasgow, all the lies. It had been the kindest thing to do. But that wouldn't have worked either. She had been right in deciding that.

When she got back to the post office, the windows were open. She could hear her parents talking.

"It's not natural," Kenneth Dance was saying. "She's my only daughter and I love her, but there's something wrong with her. What happened in Glasgow wasn't natural, and nor is this wandering round the cliffs on her own all day. She should snap herself out of it. She should think of the child, after all he's been through."

"We must be patient," Annie said. "We can't know what it was like there in Glasgow with no one to turn to."

"She could have turned to us," he shouted. "She had only to pick up a phone and we would have helped her. Why didn't she do that?"

Why didn't I? Elspeth asked herself. She had asked the same question a hundred times. Tears began to fall down her cheeks and she had to compose herself before she went in to join her parents.

George found it very difficult to persuade Elspeth to allow him to speak to Ben alone. She was happy for him to see Ben, but she wanted to be there, too. Ben seemed to be a peculiarly polite boy. He stood and listened patiently while the adults discussed him. The other children had run home, or up to Kell to watch the last of the dipping. At last Ben interrupted:

"There's no need to worry, Mummy," he said. "I'll be good. I won't chatter."

Reluctantly Elspeth went back to the post office. They watched her go.

"She does fuss," Ben said. "There's no need."

"You gave her a scarf for a present," George said. "Can you show me where you found it?"

"Of course," Ben said. Then: "It wasn't stealing, was it?"

"No. But it did belong to someone else. Can't you remember seeing Mary wearing it?"

"I do now that you've told me, but I didn't when I found it. I just thought that it was pretty."

The boy started walking along the road towards Kell and the harbour.

"I didn't go straight to school yesterday after I left home," he said. "Mummy wasn't there and Grandpa and Grandma are always busy in the mornings, because they have to be ready to open the shop. I played by myself instead."

"Where did you play?"

"In here."

They had come to the derelict croft where George had heard voices the morning before. "I came after school too, when everyone else went to watch the *Ruth Isabella* in. I pretend that it's my house," Ben said. "I come here quite often."

"You found the scarf in here?"

"Yes. In the morning. I left it here till after school." Ben led the way in through the hole in the wall which had once been a door.

"Was it hidden?"

"No. It was caught on this nail. It looked as if it had been left here by accident."

Part of the door frame was intact and a bent nail stuck from the rotting wood, at about waist height. If someone had left the building in a hurry, George thought, they might not have noticed that the scarf was left behind. The boy stood quietly by his side. It seemed not to occur to him that he might not be believed.

"What time did you get up on Saturday morning?" George asked suddenly.

"Late," Ben said, "because I was so late going to bed after the party."

"What time is late?"

"I'm not sure. I'm not very good at telling the time. It was nearly dinnertime."

"So you didn't go down to the beach or on to Ellie's Head on Saturday morning?"

"No."

"Did Mary tell you where she was going on Friday night?"

"No." He hesitated. "She was a bit bossy. I wanted to be on my own for a bit, so I hid in the toilet. I know it wasn't very nice but she'd been chasing me around all evening. When I came out she'd gone."

"Had the dancing stopped for the interval when you came out?"

"They were just stopping."

"Thank you, Ben," George said. "You've been very helpful."

The boy seemed pleased.

They walked back south down the road. They were almost at the post office when the boy touched George's arm.

"Mr. Palmer-Jones," he said, "can I ask you something?"

"Of course."

"When Mary fell," he said, "would it have hurt?"

"No," George said seriously.

"Are you sure?"

"Yes."

"That's all right then. I didn't like her very much, but I wouldn't have wanted it to hurt."

"Did she tell you what her secret was?"

"No, she talked about it a lot, but she didn't tell me what it was. I did think . . ."

"Yes?"

"Oh, nothing. I'd better go in now."

He stood briefly in front of George, shook the man's hand, then ran indoors.

At Kell they had finished dipping. It had turned into something of a party. There were more lambs than anyone had expected. Some of the men had cans of beer. They stood leaning against the sheep pen laughing and gossiping. They were in no hurry to go home. James wished that they would go. He was in no mood for gossip and laughter. Years ago it had been a great day, the Hill Gather. He and Melissa had invited everyone on Kinness into their house, when it was all finished. There had been whisky and fiddle music into the evening. Now he wanted it all to be over. All the people turned Kell into a prison for Melissa. She would not come out while they were there.

At last they began to drift away to their homes and their wives. Sarah was the first to go. She left Jim there, talking to Alec, drinking beer. George met her by the school-house gate.

"I've found the scarf," he said.

She was surprised. She thought that nonsense was all over.

"Where?" she said. "Was it down on the beach?"

"No, it was in Taft, the empty croft near the road."

"How did it get there?"

"If we knew that we would know who pushed Mary Stennet over Ellie's Head."

"So you still think that she was pushed?"

"Oh yes," he said. "Now that I've found the scarf there's no other explanation."

Chapter Eight

The next day was colder. The wild geese came, the pink-footed geese from Iceland, and the men went out to shoot them. Jim did not go. He said that he was too busy, though Sarah thought he had stayed at home to spare her feelings. She had seen the geese flying over the house and heard them calling.

Alec came to ask Jim to go with him.

"I thought you wanted to start the second-cut silage," Jim said. "There's too much to do."

"You go," Sarah said. "I don't mind."

But she was pleased when he stuck it out and insisted he was too busy.

"You're getting soft," Alec jeered. "You've been too long in the south. You'll have to come to supper one night and taste what you're missing."

It was a still, clear day. It's already winter here, Sarah thought, and in my parents' house the leaves will hardly have changed colour.

"Can I help you?" she asked Jim. He was sitting on the wooden chair by the kitchen door, pulling Wellington boots over long knitted socks. He was in a hurry because Alec had kept him talking, and he hardly looked up.

"No," he said. "There's nothing for you to do. If you're bored you could go to see Mother. She would like to see you."

Robert heard the geese and watched the men go after them. Nobody asked him to go, too. Even when he was younger he was left out of expeditions like that. They had always laughed at him. He had always been left out. It was because he had no family of his own. It would be different if he had married and he had sons to the house who said: "Father, we're off after the geese. You come with us," or daughters to cook a goose and ask him to dinner to share it.

He had always liked the girls and would have asked any one of them to marry him, but he knew that they would only laugh at him. Perhaps it was his leg, white and withered with polio, that made them laugh. Sometimes he wanted to show them that he was a man like other men, take the smiles off their pretty faces.

The geese would be on the lochan at Kell. There would be no point in going that way. Now that they all had freezers in their houses there was never a bird to be given away, no matter how many they shot. It was then that he remembered the people he had seen in Taft, on the foggy morning when the lorry broke down. That information might be worth a goose, he thought, remembering the frantic, intimate whispers. Someone might give me a goose to keep quiet about that. But that would have to wait until later. Now he would bring his wood up Ellie's Geo and begin to saw it into logs for the winter.

He was dragging one long and awkward plank down the hill to Tain when he saw the girl from Unsta, Jim Stennet's new wife. He thought how pretty she was. She'll be making all the other women jealous, he thought with satisfaction. She was sitting on Ellie's Head looking out to sea, and she did not see him. He took pleasure in watching her, without her being aware of it. Although it was so cold, she was not wearing a coat and her sweater was tight. No other woman on the island had a sweater like it, and he thought that soon they would all be searching through their mail-order catalogues to find clothes like the girl from Unsta wore. Suddenly she got up and turned to walk down the hill. She must have seen him looking at her. He turned away quickly and limped on, dragging the wood behind him.

Sarah had been thinking of Mary. It had been a shock to see the old man staring at her. She walked quicker than he did and soon caught him up.

"Can I help you?" she asked.

He was surprised. He had thought that she would be cross with him for staring, but she was so pretty that he supposed that she was used to the men looking at her. He accepted her offer of help immediately before she changed her mind. Usually he had to beg for assistance. Help on Kinness was only freely given to family.

She took one end of the plank and they walked together, carrying the wood between them, towards Tain. He did not speak. She was surprised by how strong he was. Several times she had to ask him to stop so that she could rest. When they got to the house he showed her where they could leave the plank. He stood and looked at her, smiling, twisting his flat cap between his hands. It was a peculiar smile, frankly admiring, almost innocent. He was, Sarah thought, a little strange.

"You'll take some tea?" he asked. "Or a dram?"

"I'd like some tea," she said.

He hopped into the house, followed by his dog, and held the door open for her to go in. He was obviously pleased that she had accepted his invitation, but he was awkward now and a little shy. He showed her into a small dark room which could not have changed much since he was a child. Under the window was a square table covered with oil cloth. A black cast-iron stove jutted into the room from one wall. On shelves at either side of it were some religious books, an ugly wooden clock, an ornamental plate showing the coronation of Queen Elizabeth, and an assortment of glass animals. Two high-backed chairs made from driftwood in the island pattern stood by the stove, and in one corner was a spinning wheel. The room was tidy, but dusty. The window was dirty and allowed in little light. When Robert came in from the scullery after filling the kettle, she was still looking at the spinning wheel.

"That was my mother's," he said. "She was a fine spinner. She kept the wool as even as can be and never broke the yarn."

He put the kettle on the stove. The dog, which lay on the black sheepskin hearth rug, did not look up.

"I make the best tea in Kinness," he said proudly. "It's the Tain water."

She had to concentrate to understand him. He made no concession in his speech. She sat in one of the chairs. He took the other.

"It'll take a while to boil," he said. They looked at each other for a moment in silence, and then he began to talk.

"I was sorry about the lassie," he said. "It will have spoiled your wedding party."

"I was sorry," she said, "but not because of that."

"Wasn't it peculiar that it happened on the same day as the storm? And that she fell over Ellie's Head?"

"The storm?"

That was all that it took for him to start the story. It was as if he had rehearsed what he had to say. It came out as a set piece—remembered by heart and recited when an audience could be found. Perhaps it was like that. Certainly he had told the story before—to American tourists and to a lady from the Baltasay museum who came with a tape recorder—but it seemed to Sarah that he specially wanted to tell it to her.

"I am the only one left who remembers it," he said. "I was only a boy. The men saw some French boats out to the south, and thought that they could trade with them. They would take out chicken, mutton, dried fish and bring back tea, salt, perhaps even brandy. Trading like that happened often in those days. All the men went out. They preferred to be out with the boats to staying here and working on the harvest. The harvest was late that year. It was thought to be women's work. Even boys of my age went with them, but they wouldn't let me go and I had to stay with my mother and my sisters.

"It was a fine day. We watched the men row off towards the ships. They were all in good spirits, thinking of the drams they would have there and the brandy they would bring back. I wanted to be with them. We were in the field, stacking the sheaves into stooks to dry. We were working all afternoon. Then, all of a sudden there was such a wind that all the stooks were blown flat. I have never known a wind like it, coming out of nothing. It blew all night and it was so fierce that we were frightened to go outside. Our hen house was blown right away with all the birds inside it.

The men did not come home. The wind blew the next day as strong as ever. Eventually the boats started to come back but most of the men were lost. My father was drowned, and my uncle and my brother. Some boats had just one man alive inside. Most were washed up empty. It was a terrible time.

"Most of the men that came back alive were Stennets, and the Dances who were left said that the Stennets let their men drown to save themselves. I think it was just chance. They say that the Stennets and the Dances have never been friendly since, but myself, I don't think that was caused by the storm. I remember rows between them before then. There was a lot of bad feeling when Ellie Dance went sick in the head. She was engaged to be married to Stuart, her first cousin, and he was one of the men that were lost. Perhaps it was because there were no other young men left for her to marry that she went so mad. She never seemed to sleep. She was so mad that they had to lock her up in the post office, and she howled like a chained dog. I can still remember the howling. Then one night she got loose and threw herself over the cliff. That's why it was named Ellie's Head."

At first Sarah could not believe what he was saying. It was just a good story.

"She's buried in the graveyard," she said. "When it says 'he should have been hers,' it's talking about Stuart."

"Yes."

She thought again of the note on the wedding dress:

"He should have been mine." Perhaps the Stennets had prevented Elspeth marrying Jim, just as the Dances believed that the Stennets had been responsible for the first Ellie not marrying her Stuart.

"Jim never told me about the storm," she said.

"He will know about it all the same."

"There's still ill feeling between the Stennets and the Dances, isn't there? But that couldn't have had anything to do with Mary's death."

"No," he said, almost regretfully, because it would have been such a good story. "That most just have been coincidence. Kenneth Dance says that the Stennets could run the boat better and that

89

the freight charge is too high. The Stennets say that Kenneth Dance charges too much for the things in his shop. That's how it is now. It's money that comes between them." He paused, then continued slowly: "Kenneth and Annie did name their daughter after the poor girl that went mad. That seemed an unlucky thing to me."

He got up and poured boiling water into a small china teapot.

When she got back to Unsta, George Palmer-Jones was already there, waiting for her. He was sitting outside on the wooden bench. She was not sure that she wanted to see him, but she let him in.

He took the green and white scarf from his pocket and put it on the kitchen table between them.

"I'm going to see Sandy and Agnes," he said, "to tell them that I've found the scarf, and to ask their permission to investigate their daughter's death."

I'm going to give them the responsibility for the decision, he thought. It's too much for me now.

"Have you any more idea what can have happened?" she asked.

"Whoever pushed Mary took the scarf, either before she died or afterwards. We don't know why. On Monday morning, before the boat went out, Sylvia Drysdale was talking to someone in the derelict croft next to the road. She decided to leave the island suddenly when I asked her about anyone here who might have a secret. Later the scarf was found in the croft. It looked as if it had been dropped by accident. It could have been left by Sylvia, but more likely, I should think, by whoever she was talking to."

"You couldn't recognize the voice?"

"No. It could have been a man or a woman. It's difficult to tell with a whisper. Did any of the boat crew mention having met Sylvia that morning?"

"No."

"Robert might be able to help us," George said. "He was up on the hill above the croft that morning. He might have seen or heard something. We'll go there when we've been to Sandwick."

"You want me to come with you?"

"It would be useful. It's always helpful to have two people. You might pick up something which I've missed, but I'll quite understand if you prefer not to."

"No. I'll come."

At least I can be useful to someone, she thought as she put a cold lunch on a plate for Jim and cut a sandwich for herself, then walked up the road towards Sandwick with George. Jim had not wanted her help.

They met Sandy in the yard outside the house. He was on his way into Sandwick for lunch. Sandy beamed when he saw Sarah and took her in his arms.

"George is keeping you company," he said. "Now that is good. I saw Jim working in the top field and I thought you might be lonely."

"I'd like to talk to you," George said. "But it can wait until later if your lunch is ready."

"No. Come in. Come in."

They could hear Agnes in the kitchen, but George did not ask to speak to her, too, and Sandy did not suggest it.

"Are you sure," George said, "that Mary's death was an accident?"

"She would never have killed herself." Sandy spoke quietly so that Agnes would not hear him, but he was quite firm.

"I'm not suggesting that she did."

"Then what are you saying?"

"I believe that there is a possibility that she was murdered."

"No." This time he could not control his voice, and he spoke so loudly that he shocked them. Agnes came in to see if he was ready for his food.

"Sandy," she said, "are you ill?"

"No," he said again, though not in response to her question. He looked at George again. "If you're right," he said, "it will be that Dance."

"George," Agnes said. "What is this about?"

"I don't think that Mary's death was an accident," he said.

"No," she said. "I've been thinking that too. I don't see how it could have been." It was the last response they could have expected.

She seemed so unworldly, almost simple. "But we will accuse nobody, Sandy, until we are certain."

"What made you believe that Mary was pushed?" George asked Agnes.

"She had never fallen in her life. And then there was something else. She liked to eat. Especially cakes and biscuits. If she had meant to run away to make a fuss, she would have waited until after the interval."

"You said nothing to me," Sandy said.

"It meant nothing. What could I prove? You would have said I was foolish."

"I was worried about the scarf," George said. "It should have been on her body. It was found in the old croft by Kell, on Monday morning. Someone was in there on Monday morning when I came down to see the boat off. Did you notice anything when you walked past, Sandy?"

Sandy shook his head.

"Did you tell the police about this?"

"I tried to, but they were convinced it was an accident. They had no reason to think otherwise."

"What will you do now?"

"What would you like me to do?"

"Find out."

"It won't be easy," George said. "There will be awkward questions. People won't like it."

"All the same," Sandy said, "we will find out."

"I may be mistaken."

"At least we will know."

"Have you made a will?"

Sarah was as surprised by the last question as Sandy was. At first she thought he would refuse to answer. She expected him to tell George that it was none of his business.

"Yes," Sandy said. "I've made a will."

"Could you tell me what provisions were contained in it?"

"I left Sandwick to Mary," Sandy said slowly, "the house and the croft would both belong to her. It seemed the best way to be sure that she was taken care of."

"So that if either of your sons wished to farm Sandwick and live in this house, they would have to take responsibility for Mary."

"Yes. Sandwick is her home. We didn't want her moved out to an institution as soon as we died."

"What was to happen if you were to retire?"

"The same thing. The boys knew that if they wanted to farm Sandwick they would have to take care of Mary."

"Who will inherit Sandwick now?"

"Alec. He is the eldest son." He was trying to answer the questions reasonably, but he was beginning to become angry. "Mr. Palmer-Jones," he said, "none of my family would murder a child for a house."

George ignored the anger.

"I spoke to Mary at the harbour on Friday and she talked about a secret. Do you know what that secret might have been?"

"It will just have been child's talk," Sandy said impatiently.

"There's nothing, no matter how trivial, which might have interested her, that I don't want to know about. She seemed very excited when she spoke to me."

He was appealing to Sandy and to Agnes. Sarah thought that Sandy was going to speak, but Agnes looked at her husband carefully, seemed to warn him.

"No," he said. "There's nothing."

They prepared to go.

"There's just one thing," George said. "Why do think it was Dance?"

Sandy said nothing, and it was Agnes who answered.

"Superstition," she said, "and a lack of Christian charity."

When Sarah and George left Sandwick, they went to Tain, but the house was empty. George was surprised because Robert's dog was tethered to a line outside and usually it went everywhere with the old man.

She planned a special meal for Jim that night. When he came in, he did not ask her why she was not home at lunchtime. He presumed that Agnes had asked her to stay at Sandwick. She was excited because of the conversation with Sandy and Agnes. It did not occur to her that he might be upset to hear that his sister had been murdered. She could not take it seriously. It was still a game to her.

"Agnes thinks that Mary was murdered," she said.

"Poor mother," Jim said, "I thought she was taking it very calmly. She must be hysterical."

"No," Sarah said. "George thinks that she's probably right. It's something to do with the green scarf Mary was wearing not being found on the body."

"He shouldn't encourage Mother," Jim said. "He'll make her ill."

He was not upset to think that Mary had been murdered. Quite simply he did not believe it. He began talking about the rabbits and the damage that they had done on the island. Mary was not mentioned again.

"Perhaps I'll go out with a gun later," he said.

"It'll soon be dark," she said. Then, because she wanted to finish the preparation for the meal and to get changed: "Go now then, before it's too late and I can finish the supper."

When he came back it was nearly dark, but she had not switched on the electric light. She had put a tablecloth—a wedding present—on the kitchen table, and a candle in the middle of it. He stood just inside the door and she was afraid that he would laugh at the effort she had made. But he did not laugh. He went into the bedroom and fetched a bottle of wine, brought from the mainland. She lit the candle and he opened the wine.

"I met Robert today," she said. "He gave me tea. He's very interesting."

"He's a simple-minded fool. What was he telling you?"

"He was talking about the big storm."

"Was he?"

"Why hadn't you told me about it?"

"It didn't come up. Perhaps I thought that you wouldn't understand."

"I don't think I would have done, away from Kinness. Did you know that Elspeth was named after Ellie, who went mad and drowned herself?"

"Of course. I was brought up with it."

They were sitting at the table, drinking the wine. It seemed to Sarah that the conversation was important to Jim. When he came into the house after shooting the rabbits, he had seemed different, as if he had made up his mind about something. It was quite dark outside now. She stared out of the window. There were a couple of lights on the horizon—boats, she supposed—but otherwise there was a dense, deep darkness. It's never this dark on the mainland, she thought. There's always a light somewhere, even if it's the reflected glow of a town miles away, or car headlights.

"I was brought up with it," Jim repeated. "We all were. The story of Ellie. The fact that very few Dances survived. Perhaps that was what attracted me to Elspeth. I thought that we would get married and that the island would be brought together again."

She waited for him to tell her more about Elspeth, but he said nothing.

"Robert thinks the feud has nothing to do with the storm now," she said. "He says it's all about freight charges and shop prices."

"Perhaps he's not so simple-minded after all."

There was another silence.

"I want to tell you about Elspeth."

"Robert told me you were going to be married. Were you engaged?

"No. It was nothing like that. Nothing formal. We were both very young."

He poured himself more wine.

"She's a year older than me, so she went out to school in Baltasay before I did. I never got to know her at school. She was living in the hostel and by that time I had lodgings with one of Maggie's aunts. It was one summer. I was the same age as Will is now and we were both here on Kinness. She was lively, fun, and I suddenly realized how pretty she was. She'd applied to go to drama school in Glasgow, though she hadn't heard then whether or not she'd got in ... It was a lovely summer. Hot for here. And in early summer it's light nearly all night. I can't remember helping much on the croft. Every day I was out with Elspeth. We swam and walked, and talked for hours and hours. She read me bits of plays. I didn't understand them, but I loved to hear her do all the voices. She was older than me. She was an only child, and I suppose the Dances had more money to spend on her. She used to go and stay in Glasgow with friends Kenneth had made there, and once she spent a month in France learning the language. She seemed stylish and sophisticated.

"I started making plans for the future. I'd always wanted to go to agricultural college, but I thought that if I worked hard and got my exams I might get to university in Glasgow, too. I could study agriculture there. I imagined being sophisticated, too.

"Then, well before the end of the holiday, she went. She didn't tell me that she was going. A plane came in very early and she went out with it. There was no letter, nothing.

"It turned out that there was a man in Glasgow, and that she was pregnant, though I didn't know that then. The baby wasn't mine. There was nothing between us but passionate kisses in the moonlight and the occasional grope in the barn. Later she got married. It was a quiet wedding and I wasn't invited.

"After she left I went a bit wild. There didn't seem any point in working for exams anymore. I was still staying with Maggie's auntie on Baltasay for my last year of school, but I got in with a different crowd—lads who'd already left school. I went out drinking with them. Then I got thrown out of the lodging. There was some trouble with the police. I made a fool of myself.

"All the time I was writing to her, trying to find out what had happened. Kenneth and Annie wouldn't say anything. I even went down to Glasgow once.

"Then she wrote to me and told me what had happened. I remember the letter coming. I was home for the Christmas holidays. She explained about the baby. It was a peculiar letter, but she said that she was happy. It was full of all the things she was doing at college—parties, rehearsals. She carried on there although she must have been quite pregnant by then. She didn't tell me anything about the baby's father.

"They let me stay on at school but I didn't do very well in the exams."

All the time he was talking he was staring out of the window. He turned to face his wife.

"I was obsessed by the fact that she must have been pretending for the whole of that summer."

She stretched out and took his hand.

"I'm glad you told me about her."

"I should have told you before. I didn't know that she'd be here."

"I realized that. What happened to her husband?"

"They're divorced. There's just her and the child."

He had never talked to her so intimately before. She felt very close to him. With the same ridiculous, romantic impulse which had made her dream of Kinness as paradise, she was certain that now everything would be happy between them.

George waited in the school house until Jonathan had finished teaching. That day the island had seemed full of frenzied activity, as the men chased the geese in Alec's battered car. He supposed that Robert must be with them. He did not want to approach them to find out, so he decided that he would talk to Jonathan. If Sylvia was hiding something, her husband must suspect it. When the school bell rang to send the children home, he made a pot of tea, and waited in the kitchen for the teacher to come in.

Jonathan looked tired.

"Maggie Stennet was waiting for me again," he said. "She's been trying to find out how long Sylvia will be away."

"How long *will* Sylvia be on Baltasay?"

"I don't know."

"Has she phoned?"

"Yes."

"Why did she leave the island so suddenly?"

"I don't know."

"You must have some idea."

Drysdale remained silent.

"Was it my talk of secrets?"

"It's none of your business!" For a moment he lost control.

George spoke quietly and calmly. "I explained my concern about the disappearance of Mary's scarf. It was found on Monday. I think Sylvia was talking to the person who dropped it before she got on to the boat. If you know anything you must tell me."

"Really. I don't know anything."

"Did you walk some of the way with Sylvia on Monday morning?"

"No."

"Why not?"

"She said not to bother. We'd arranged for Alec to pick up her luggage."

"What happened to make you both so unhappy?"

"I told you. She's bored here."

"Why does Maggie Stennet dislike Sylvia so much?"

It was a stab in the dark, a wild guess, but at last he provoked a reaction.

"Because Maggie's a venomous bitch. It's not Sylvia's fault that Alec Stennet chases every woman under forty on the island."

"Was Sylvia having an affair with. Alec?"

"No!" He was shouting. "She flirted with him. I've told you. She was bored. She flirted with every man on Kinness."

He stood up, said that he was going for a walk, and went out.

In Kell, Melissa waited for James. She did not mind that he had been out all day. She knew that he enjoyed the companionship of the other men. She was not much company now. He was a good shot, too, and always came back with more birds than the others. But she knew that she was spending more and more time alone, and knew that it did her no good. I must make the effort, she thought, or I'll go mad like poor Ellie Dance, and start howling at the moon like a dog.

Ben had been late home from school again, very late, and Elspeth had begun to panic.

"He shouldn't go running about the island by himself. Look what happened to Mary Stennet. It's dangerous, especially with the men firing like wild things at anything that moves."

"You should have gone to collect him," Annie said.

"I know, but he does hate it. He says that only the babies are collected by their mothers. And it's only up the road."

"Just the same. I think you should collect him."

"I will. Every day. If only he's safe."

Kenneth had gone out in the end to look for him, and had found him squatting in the tumbledown croft, writing on the dirt floor, apparently oblivious to time.

"What are you doing?" Kenneth asked.

"I was making a spell."

Maggie hated it when Alec was so pleased with himself. He came in at last, after the boys were in bed, stinking of drink and boasting of what a brilliant shot he was.

"Where have you been?" she demanded. She was furious.

"I've been having a few drinks," he said, "to celebrate."

"Your father should know better than to get you in this state. There'll be time to celebrate when you've cut the silage. What have you got to celebrate?"

Alec sat down carefully.

"He's talking," he said, "about retiring."

George Palmer-Jones went to bed early. Jonathan Drysdale had come back from his walk in a peculiar, feverish state and had talked all evening about whooper swans. He had been up to Silver Water, and the whooper swans were there. This year he was determined to ring them. They would do it soon, and George must help him. George found the frightened, relentless conversation sad and exhausting and went to bed to escape it. At first he did not sleep, and when the generator went off he was still awake, making plans for the next day.

He must eventually have slept, because the howls of the dog pierced his dreams, and when he woke, he thought he must still be dreaming. It was a horrible chilling noise and it sounded very close to the house. He could not believe that Jonathan was sleeping through it. It continued, high-pitched and disturbing. He tried to go back to sleep, but it was impossible. He thought that perhaps the dog had been hit by a stray shot, and finally he got up and dressed and went outside. There was a very thin moon but he needed a torch to see. The noise came from the low, boggy area of the Loons. He splashed across the drainage ditches and swore as the water trickled into his Wellingtons. The whole thing was foolish. He should have stayed in bed.

Then he saw the dog. It had not been shot. But Robert, lying beside it, had been dead for hours. He lay on his back and his face and the dog were covered in blood. There was no clean bullet wound. He had been killed, like the geese, with a shotgun. The dog, which had accompanied him everywhere, had broken free from his line and found him at last.

It was a shock, of course, and quite terrible, but George felt relief, too. I was right, he thought. The child was murdered. This proves it.

Chapter Nine

The next morning, as soon as it was light, the police flew in. George borrowed Jonathan's car and went to the airstrip to meet them. There were the same two officers who had come to Kinness before. They were confused and unhappy—they did not want the responsibility of coming to a decision about violent death—but George soon lost patience with them. They would not agree that Mary and Robert had been murdered. He took them to the body. It was still where he had found it the night before. He had woken Jonathan and together they had covered it with tarpaulin, but they had not moved it.

The elder policeman, the inspector, was near to retirement. He had a mainland accent. Perhaps he had moved to Baltasay for the peace.

"So they were shooting geese here yesterday?" he said.

"Yes."

"All day?"

"On and off. I heard them in the morning and again in the afternoon at about three."

The inspector turned to his colleague.

"I suppose it couldn't have been an accident?"

The younger man had been born on Baltasay.

"It could have been," he said, "but someone would have seen it happen. Why not report it? Try to get help for the old man."

"It couldn't have been an accident," George said. "Robert had information about Mary Stennet's death."

This was too much for them. They were convinced that Mary

Stennet had fallen accidentally. They had put in their reports to that effect.

"When was the old man last seen?" the constable asked, quickly changing the subject.

"I know that Sarah Stennet was talking to him yesterday morning. We went to his house yesterday afternoon, but he wasn't there then."

"That would tie in with the accident theory, then. If he was away from home when the men were up here shooting."

"He was murdered," George said, with such certainty and authority that they deferred to him, accepted his judgement.

"It certainly seems that way," the inspector said, "but it's not the sort of decision we can make on the spot. We'll have to take a statement of course, then report back to headquarters."

"While you're doing that," George said, "you won't object if I try to find out what happened."

He left them standing in the marsh, wondering how best to move the body. Furious with the defective logic, their inability to think clearly, his own ineffectiveness, he walked down the island and banged on the door at Unsta. He was determined now to finish the thing quickly. He had to prove to himself and to the police now that he could do it. He had wasted five days. Sarah came to the door. It was still early, but Jim was already out.

"Robert's been murdered," he said.

She felt betrayed. The evening before had promised endless happiness. The promise was already broken.

"The police are trying to persuade themselves that it was another accident," he said. "It's just intellectual laziness. They'll realize that soon. I want to ask some questions before they start taking statements. Will you come with me?"

He was compelling. He made her feel that it was her duty to go with him. He seemed to have a new energy and power. When they walked she found it hard to keep up with him. Yet he had had no sleep.

He was unsure why he was so reluctant to ask the questions alone. When he was working as a civil servant with the Home

Office, there had been no opportunity to share responsibility. His independence had been the aspect of the work he had enjoyed most. Perhaps he had become too accustomed to sharing problems with Molly. He knew that an extra perspective would be invaluable.

"I wouldn't want to put you in an awkward position."

"No. I'd like to come with you. I think I should."

His power and authority attracted her.

"I thought that we'd start at Kell and move south."

"I understood that visitors weren't welcomed at Kell."

His sudden burst of anger surprised her: "We won't behave like the foolish policemen," he said. "We're doing the thing properly. If you prefer you can opt out now."

"No. I want to come."

He talked continuously as they walked, communicating his thoughts to her, and ordering his ideas, so that he would know just what questions to ask.

"Robert found out Mary's secret," he said. "He saw or heard something, or he worked it out for himself. He saw the person talking to Sylvia Drysdale, but that might mean nothing. We must remember it, but not give it undue importance. If we knew the secret, we would know the identity of the murderer. It's the essence of the case. But several people here seem to have a secret. Maggie thinks that Alec and Sylvia were having an affair. Elspeth Dance is frightened of something. She was afraid that her son would talk to me. Kenneth and Annie are trying to protect her. Jonathan says that Sylvia flirted with anyone who would give her attention, so she might have been involved with more than one man."

"Might there not be another motive?" she interrupted nervously. "The secret might just have been a game."

"You're right, of course," he said. "There's Sandy's will, for example. We must keep an open mind about motives."

But he was convinced that the secret was essential.

When they reached Kell, Sarah was hot and breathless. There were no geese left on the low land in front of the croft, and the lochan was as still and blue as the sea beyond. James was sawing wood just outside the house. He was in his shirt sleeves, and as he heard them approaching and looked up to watch them, he wiped his forehead with a clean, white handkerchief.

"Hello," he said cautiously. George was wearing binoculars as he always did, and James continued. "Is there some rare bird on my land that I've not heard about? You know that you're welcome to go where you please."

"No," George said. "We wanted to talk to you. Had you heard that Robert was dead?"

"No," James said. He seemed shocked but made no pretence at grief. "And he seemed so healthy. Was it a heart attack? I heard the plane. I suppose that will have been the doctor. Of course he had no family left."

Family, Sarah thought, why should family be so important? Kinness was so small, they should all consider each other as family.

"The doctor didn't come in the plane," George said. "It was the police. He was shot."

James put down the saw slowly.

"What happened?" he asked.

"I don't know. The police think it may have been an accident. Could we go inside? I'd like to ask some questions. It's about Mary. I'd like Melissa to hear about it, too."

James looked embarrassed and anxious. He did not like to refuse George, but he had to think about Melissa. The habit of protecting her had become a way of life.

"I don't know," he said. "She seems to have been a lot better recently, but I don't want to rush things. She doesn't find it easy to talk to strangers."

Melissa was watching them through the kitchen window. They represented the world away from Kell. They were normal people and suddenly she wanted to be normal, too. The kettle was nearly boiling on the stove. She threw open the kitchen window, and before she had the chance to change her mind she shouted:

"Bring your friends in, James. Don't keep them standing out there in the cold. I'm making some tea."

She felt hot with triumph and excitement. She turned and laid out her best cups and saucers on the table, and poured milk from the churn in the scullery into a jug.

Sarah had seen Melissa in the church, but there had been many strangers there that day, and she had not looked closely at her new aunt. Now Melissa impressed her. With her dark hair and eyes and white skin, she could have been Russian or Polish. There was still no trace of the island accent in her voice.

James showed them into the kitchen. He sat them at the table, as far away as possible from Melissa. She seemed well, but she did not like to be crowded and he was worried that they might provoke one of her panic attacks. He was so concerned about her that he seemed not to have considered what George might want with them. George was beginning to wonder if perhaps he should have agreed to talk to James alone. He thought it unlikely that Melissa was the murderer—she had not even been at the dance. Now he felt restrained because of her fragility. How could he speak directly about death when she seemed to have lived so little?

James spoke first.

"Old Robert's dead," he said gently. "He was shot."

"Who shot him?" Melissa asked immediately.

James looked at George for more information.

"The police don't know," George said. "You didn't hear anything?"

"No. We wouldn't do. We go to bed very early."

"You were out shooting yesterday with the men?" George asked James.

"Yes."

"Did you see Robert then?"

"No."

"What time did you finish?"

"I don't know the time exactly. When the light began to go."

There was a silence.

"Why have you come?" Melissa asked. "You told James it was about Mary."

"It is about Mary," George said. "I don't believe that her death was an accident."

He had spoken softly and he thought she had not heard him.

"I think that the girl was murdered," he said.

"I heard you," she said. "What is going on here? An old man shot and a girl murdered. What do you want from us?"

While George was talking to Melissa, Sarah was watching James. He was horrified, as if he could not believe that they could discuss a child's death so calmly.

"You're wrong," he said. "No one here would commit that sort of violence. This is Kinness."

"All the same," George said. "I'm quite sure."

"No. I won't have it." He sat down at the table next to George. "I'm the nearest thing there is to a minister here. People come to talk to me. I know them. There is no one here who would kill a child."

Was the horror because Mary was a child, Sarah wondered, or did James care so much more about her than Robert because she was a Stennet and Robert was not?

"It would help to convince me if you would answer some questions."

"I'll answer any question you like, but it'll make no difference."

Melissa was surprised that she felt so calm. It had been years since they had entertained strangers in the house, but she felt none of the usual panic. She listened with a detached and intense concentration to George's questions and her husband's answers.

"Mary liked and trusted you. Did she talk to you about a secret at the dance on Friday night?"

"No. I hardly saw her at all on Friday night."

"You were playing with the band for most of the evening. What did you do in the interval?"

"It was rowdy in the hall. I didn't want to take any drink, but I didn't want to seem a kill joy. I went outside, just for some fresh air."

"Where did you go?"

"I didn't go anywhere. I stood outside the hall."

"Did you see anyone?"

"There were a lot of people who came outside like me. I saw some women taking their children home. I saw this young woman." He nodded disapprovingly at Sarah. She remembered how drunk she had been and felt ashamed.

George continued: "Did you see Sylvia Drysdale? Was she outside?"

He hesitated and Sarah thought that he was going to ask a question, but James only shook his head.

"What do you know about Sylvia Drysdale?"

The question was meant for James, but Melissa answered: "She's sad. Sad and lonely."

"How did you know her?" Sarah asked gently. "You don't leave Kell very often."

"She came to see me a few times when she moved on to the island. She was interested in spinning and weaving, and especially the old vegetable dyes which the women used to colour the wool. James' mother told me how the dyes were made. I was interested in it myself at one time. Agnes never bothered much with it. She never had the time, with the children to look after. So James' mother passed all her recipes to me. I was pleased to talk to Sylvia. I looked forward to her visits. Then suddenly she stopped coming. She never told me why. I suppose she just lost interest." She looked at her husband. "I asked James to go to see her, to ask her to start visiting again, but he wouldn't do it."

James looked uncomfortable.

"She has something of a reputation," he said. "I felt awkward about going there to see her."

"You never used to mind what people were thinking."

There was a pause in the conversation. James and Melissa seemed engrossed in thoughts of their own. Sarah looked out to the hill and as she watched six swans flew over, honking, and disappeared below the horizon. George had seen them, too, but did not want to be distracted.

"Sylvia Drysdale met someone on the way to the *Ruth Isabella* on Monday," he said. "It may be important. Taft isn't far from here. You didn't see who she was talking to?"

"No," James said. "Why didn't you ask her?"

"She says that she didn't speak to anyone. I think she's lying."

"She wouldn't lie," Melissa said. "Sylvia wouldn't lie."

James turned on her. "You don't know," he said angrily. "She's a wicked woman."

"Whoever was talking to her," George said, "dropped this." He pulled the green scarf from his pocket. "Do you know anything about it?"

But James' anger seemed to have unbalanced Melissa. She started to breathe very quickly as if she were short of air, and she was pale. She seemed not to be listening.

"You've upset her," James said. "You'll have to go."

Melissa was fighting for control. She had begun to weep.

George stood up. "I'm sorry," he said. "You have helped us."

Sarah spoke directly to Melissa: "I'm interested in spinning and weaving," she said. "If you feel like talking to me, tell James to let me know, and I'll come and visit."

James was desperate now to get them out of the house. He walked with them into the yard.

"You shouldn't have come," he said. "I knew that you would make her ill." His face was grey with anxiety. "Please don't come back."

In the kitchen Melissa stood up and walked to the window. She stood watching the three people in the yard and her breathing became more regular. She was furious with her weakness. It was more important than ever to stay strong. She could feel the tears stinging on her cheeks, and wiped them away with her apron. James came back into the kitchen and turned to face her. He looked anxious and apologetic. She held out her hands to him. He approached her cautiously, afraid of being rejected yet again. She held him tight, ferociously tight, then she kissed him.

Sarah followed George down the road from Kell. He walked very quickly. They did not speak. George seemed preoccupied and Sarah was afraid of interrupting his thoughts. The interview had shaken her. She had been shocked by Melissa's sudden spasm of panic. Alec's car was parked on the road near Robert's body and

George supposed that the policemen had sought his help in moving it. He hurried past, worried that the police might detain him. When he and Sarah were out of sight he stopped, took out a field notebook, leant it against a drystone wall, and wrote in it.

"I can't rely on memory," he said, "and I find it helps to put things in perspective."

"I'm sorry," she said. "I don't understand what you would need to write down. We didn't learn anything new, did we?"

He looked at her seriously. "It was most useful," he said.

"Tell me," she said.

"Oh no. I don't think so. Not yet."

"Why did you let them think that the police are convinced that Robert's death was an accident?"

"They might talk more freely." He looked at his watch. "We'll go to the post office now."

The post office was shut—it was shut all day on Thursday. They went to the private front door of the house and George knocked on it. Annie opened the door to them. She was small and neat. She had a quiet voice.

"I'm sorry," she said. "The shop is shut today. Is it urgent?"

"We don't want the shop," Sarah said.

She still did not understand. "I could let you have some stamps, but it won't do any good. The mail won't leave Kinness until Saturday."

"I'd like to talk to you and Kenneth," George said. "And to Elspeth if she's here."

Annie opened the door to them.

"We're all in here," she said, showing them into the kitchen. "I have an order of knitwear to go south. I supply a big department store in Edinburgh."

It seemed to Sarah that she was very shy. The kitchen table was piled with gloves, mittens, and hats. Elspeth was checking the goods against the order form and Kenneth was packing them into boxes. She supposed that the child was at school.

"I have a machine," Annie said, as if to explain the productivity.

It would be wrong to allow them to believe that she had knitted the garments. Knitting was a skill she took seriously. "I only handknit jerseys for private orders."

Kenneth was bending over a box on the kitchen floor, and Sarah could see that he had a shiny bald patch on his head. He looked up and stared at her.

"If you've come to buy knitwear," he said, "you're unlucky. All this has to go south."

"We don't want to buy anything," George said. "Have you heard about Robert?"

Kenneth got up from his knees and sat on one of the wooden chairs.

"Yes. I saw Alec earlier. Do you know what happened? No one seems to know exactly."

"The police seem to think it was a terrible accident. Were you out shooting yesterday?"

"Yes. I was out with the others. But I didn't see Robert. I don't know how anyone could have come to hit him."

Nor do I, George thought.

"I want to talk to you about Mary Stennet," he said. "I think that she was murdered."

"Is that what they're saying now, that she was murdered?" Dance almost spat out the words in his scorn. He turned to Sarah. "And who do they blame for this 'murder'?"

"The Stennets accuse no one for her murder."

George had raised his voice, and interrupted Dance. There was silence. He continued, speaking more softly:

"She was pushed from Ellie's Head. I will discover who did that. I want you to help me."

They seemed stunned. Again there was no reply. Elspeth was playing with a lock of her curly hair. She was watching them intently like a child watching adults, waiting for them to reach a decision. It seeemed to Sarah that she was frightened.

"How terrible," Annie said. "The poor deaf child."

"Did you see her leave the party on Friday night?" Once again George's words demanded their attention. He looked at them each in turn. Annie shook her head. "I remember seeing her dancing and thinking how she was enjoying herself, but I didn't notice that she was missing until Agnes started to cry."

George turned to Elspeth.

"Do you know why anyone would have wanted Mary dead?" he asked.

"Why do you ask me that?" The answer was unexpected, peculiarly defensive, as if he had accused her of the crime. "I wouldn't harm a child. I have a child of my own."

"How long have you been back on Kinness?" George asked with quiet interest. Elspeth was behaving so strangely that she became a focus of interest in her own right. Any information she had about Mary's movements could wait.

"About six months."

"Your son is at school here. Do you plan to stay?"

"I don't know. I'm not committed to anything." She spoke quickly and her eyes moved from George to her father.

"What's that got to do with anything?" Kenneth Dance demanded. "That's nothing to do with Mary Stennet."

"No. It has nothing to do with her." He turned back to Elspeth. "Did you see Mary at the party? Did you see her leave?"

"No," she said. "I didn't. Ben was with her at the beginning of the evening. Then Agnes asked me to sing in the interval. I didn't see Mary again."

"So you can't help me?"

"Not really. I can't. I would help you if I could. I'm sorry." The answer was too emphatic, but George turned to her father.

"Did you notice the child at the party?"

"I probably saw her, but I was playing with the band."

"What did you do during the interval?"

"Nothing. I fancied a can of beer, but there was none. I had a cup of tea."

"You didn't leave the hall, then?"

"No. I've told you."

Again Elspeth's eyes flickered towards her father.

George watched them, convinced that they had something to

hide, wishing that he could penetrate their mistrust. Sarah found the silence awkward. It was obvious that they were not wanted. She stood up, and reluctantly George followed. She went through the door first, but she still heard Kenneth Dance say to George in a low, conversational voice:

"I shouldn't go prying into other folks' affairs if I were you. You might get hurt."

Outside in the bright cold light George made no reference to the threat.

"My wife used to be a social worker," he said. "I miss her expertise at times like these. Elspeth's very unhappy, don't you think?"

"Yes," Sarah said. "Very."

She asked George to Unsta for lunch.

"Jim will be there," she said. "You can talk to him."

"I don't want to intrude."

"It won't be an intrusion. Besides, he was out yesterday evening. Alone. With a shotgun."

He said nothing. She would have preferred some reassurance, an insistence that Jim could not be under suspicion.

Jim was washing his hands in the kitchen sink when they arrived. He was angry. The police had spoken to him. They had implied that the islanders were negligent in their use of firearms, that they were trigger happy, that someone had been shooting in bad light, and that Robert had been hit without anyone noticing.

"It's impossible," Jim said. "Everyone here knows what they're doing."

"I agree," George said. "It's impossible."

Sarah put on the kettle and began to fry bacon and eggs. The men sat at the kitchen table.

"Did you see Robert when you were out yesterday?" George asked.

"Yes. I was up on the top field and you can see Tain from there. He walked north up the road."

"You were shooting rabbits?"

"No. Not then. That was later."

"What time did you see Robert?"

Jim shrugged. "Soon after lunch."

"Did you see anyone when you were out with your gun?"

"No." Jim leaned back in his chair. "I didn't kill him," he said. "I stayed on my own land. I didn't go near to the Loons."

"Do you know what secret Mary had?" George asked suddenly. "She mentioned it at the harbour and again at the party. It wasn't a child's game, forgotten in five minutes. What could it have been?"

"There's no privacy here," Jim said. "The most trivial thing a person wants to keep to himself becomes a secret."

Sarah was carrying plates of food to the table.

"What about you?" she asked. "Do you have a secret?"

"No," he said. "Not me."

As they ate George asked Jim the questions which had become routine: when had he last seen Mary at the party, had he left the hall at any time, had he noticed anybody else leave the hall, had he seen anyone talking to Sylvia Drysdale on boat day? Jim answered courteously but he had nothing to add. He was no real help.

As soon as the questions were over George was impatient to move on. If the policemen were moving down the island, there was a danger that they might get to Buness before he did. Jim watched impassively as Sarah rushed to clear the plates and followed George out.

When they arrived at Buness, Maggie was baking. Alec was still out. She had wanted a proper kitchen, separate from the living room, and it had been built on the back of the house. It was long and thin like a corridor. She was keading bread dough and her plain freckled face was red. Sarah remembered that Alec had said that Maggie was up early on the boat morning to bake, and thought she must spend very little time out of the kitchen. When they knocked on the kitchen door, she called them in without stopping the stretching and pressing of the dough. George remarked politely that the bread would be good when it was cooked. She cut it into three, rolled it in flour.

"I bake all my own bread. I wouldn't buy from the shop the

prices he charges. I'll be finished just now, then I'll make some tea."

She covered the loaves with a tea towel, rinsed her hands under the tap, then led George and Sarah into the living room. It was intimidating in its tidiness. Every surface was highly polished. There was a large sofa covered with nylon velvet and a glass-topped coffee table. They sat down and she went out to make tea. She had left open the living-room door and they heard Alec call into the kitchen.

"Robert's dead," they heard him say, "he always was a mischief-making old fool, and he's still causing trouble. The police may come to see you. Don't tell them anything."

She spoke more quietly. She did not think that her guests could hear them.

"What would I tell them?" she said bitterly. "You never talk to me. What happened to Robert?"

But he had gone.

She came into the living room carrying a tray, and there was still desperation in her voice.

"Is it just a social visit?" she asked. The words were directed at Sarah, who looked at George to help her out, but he seemed not to notice.

"We did want to talk to you," she said at last, "about Mary. George thinks that she might have been murdered."

"Is this some sort of joke?" Maggie demanded. "Is this your southern sense of humour?"

"No . . ." Sarah wanted to explain, but Maggie would not let her finish. Her face, already flushed, turned scarlet. Her fury was directed at George.

"What do you mean by coming here and making trouble like this? Are you sick?"

George spoke quietly.

"It's happened again," he said. "Robert was murdered."

She did not know what to say. George took advantage of her confusion.

"Why do you dislike Sylvia Drysdale?"

"She's never fitted in here."

"Alec likes her, though?"

"Who told you that?" She was furious. He let the matter drop.

"We've talked to Sandy and Agnes," Sarah said. "They want George to find out what happened to Mary."

"They're fools to themselves."

"All the same," George said. "You will talk to us."

"I'll talk to you, but it'll do no good."

In that she was right. She had spent most of the wedding party in the kitchen, she said. Mary was supposed to help her, but she had always been unreliable. Maggie had left the hall for a few minutes to get some air during the interval, but had seen nothing suspicious. There were lots of people coming and going. Then she had asked Agnes where Mary had been and all the fuss had started. As soon as they had drunk their tea, George and Sarah left.

Outside in the road Alec had the lorry's bonnet up and was fiddling with the engine. He heard them coming, stood up, smiled lewdly at Sarah.

"Got your chaperon?" he said. "That's a pity."

"Where are the police?" George asked.

"Taking statements, they said. I lent them my car. It saves me having to hang around with them."

"I haven't seen them yet," Sarah said. "Perhaps I'd better go home."

"Yes," George said. He was quite happy for her to go. Alec watched her walk away down the road, whistled softly under his breath.

"Did you talk to Sylvia Drysdale in Taft on Monday morning?" George asked.

"Wouldn't you like to know?" Alec gave a last, lingering look at Sarah, then turned his attention back to the lorry.

"I need to know," George said. "Two people have died. I need to know what was going on between you and Sylvia Drysdale."

Alec stood up. He was balancing the spanner in his hand as if it were a weapon.

"Let the police do their own dirty work, he said. "Whatever

happens on Kinness has nothing to do with you. You might bully other folk into answering your questions, but you'll not bully me."

Deliberately he turned his back on George once more.

As George walked back towards the school house the plane took off from the airstrip. He was glad to see the police go. Their presence had only added to the pressure. The men had irritated him. But he had expected them to consult him before they left, and he felt belittled because they had ignored him.

That night Sarah found it hard to sleep. She sensed in the islanders a deep panic. Life on Kinness ran according to routine. It was ruled by certainty. People did what was expected of them, according to the season and the weather and what they heard in the kirk. There was no longer any certainty. Murder broke a rule so fundamental that they might almost believe that other laws could be broken—that they would not bother to take the boat out to Baltasay, that they would not work together on the harvest, that the kirk would be empty on Sunday. As she had rushed round with George she had felt the islanders' fear. They regarded their neighbours and even their families with suspicion. They're like children, she thought, who lose their innocence. She remembered the newspaper article she had first read about Kinness. Now paradise had been lost.

Chapter Ten

George received no news from the police the next day. Would it have been different, he wondered, if I were doing this for a living, if I were being paid for it? Perhaps then there would be more resentment from the authorities and the job would be even more difficult. At about nine o'clock a plane came in. He expected that it would be the police, and when Alec's car went past the school house towards the airstrip, the theory was confirmed, but the women who had brought their children to school, and stood gossiping in an excited huddle, told him that it was the Woollie Man.

No one knew why he was called the Woollie Man—none of the clothes he brought into the island were made of real wool. Perhaps the islanders thought he must come from Woolworth's, because that was the only cheap department store many of them had heard of. He was Sikh. No one knew his real name and he seemed not to mind. He arrived in his chartered plane every autumn, laden with goods to sell as in old days traders from the East must have arrived in Europe with silk and spices. In his boxes and suitcases there were denim jeans, cheap jersey dresses, nylon underwear, and machine-washable sweaters, but to the islanders they seemed just as exotic. He hired the hall and piled the trestle tables with his wares. He put a screen in one corner to make a changing room, because he knew that he would sell none of the skirts and dresses unless the women could try them on. He had a Glasgow accent, and a slick patter laced with good-natured humour, as he tempted his customers to buy the cheap, gaudy things.

If anyone other than Robert had died, the Woollie Man's visit would have been cancelled. Mourning was taken seriously on

Kinness. But Robert had no family left to ensure that the proprieties were observed and no one else felt able to take responsibility. In many ways it was as if the death had never happened. There was no one left to grieve for him. And perhaps they were comforted by the visit. This was one law which had not been broken and they clung to that. The Woollie Man came every autumn to Kinness. So everyone went to the hall as they always did, even those who had no intention of buying. The Woollie Man brought a touch of excitement, a flavour of a different world. Some of the mothers had kept their children away from school just so that they could see him. They brought their offspring to the hall to see the Woollie Man as if he were Father Christmas in his grotto, then sent them back to their lessons.

Will Stennet sat in the aeroplane next to the Woollie Man and felt foolish. He had always believed himself to be independent, yet he had allowed his mother to persuade him to return home without argument. He had been away for less than a week, and had just begun to enjoy the social life at school again. She had telephoned to the hostel the night before and told him she had arranged a place for him on the Woollie Man's plane. To be summoned home now was the worst kind of deprivation: He would have to make it clear to his mother immediately that he did not intend to stay, but he knew that the task would be difficult and he felt sulky and resentful.

Sandy and Agnes went with Alec to meet the plane. Agnes was desperate to see Will again. She wanted all her children near her. Robert's death seemed to have shaken her calm and stability. She knew that it was illogical but she wanted Will at Sandwick so that she could see that he was safe. The house was so empty with Mary gone. It felt unnatural. She wanted a child to mother. Alec thought that his mother was being ridiculous.

"You're mad," Alec said, glad to have something to shout about. "There's not enough work on Kinness for the men who are here."

"Your father will retire soon," she said. "Will can work the Sandwick land."

"That's crazy. He doesn't know, anything about farming. He

doesn't care. He's only interested in birds and books and music. He doesn't want to live on Kinness. He wants to go away to college. It would be disastrous."

But Agnes had persuaded herself that Will wanted to live on the island, and it was only the lack of work and opportunity which had prevented him. Sandy felt miserable. He wanted to see Will at home, but he did not feel ready to retire. He still had plans for Sandwick. He thought that Agnes was making a big mistake. The plane arrived almost immediately. Sandy watched as Agnes leaned out of the car window, trying to get the first glimpse of her son. Then she was out of the car and hurrying over the short grass to meet Will. Sadly, Sandy got out of the car and followed her.

The three of them stood making awkward conversation, stamping their feet because although the sun was shining it was very cold, while Alec helped to unload the plane. There was not enough room for all of them in the car, so Alec drove away with the Woollie Man and his wares, leaving them on the windswept sheep-grazed hill. Will slouched gracelessly, and scuffed the grass with his boots. He had intended, as soon as he arrived, telling Agnes that his stay would only be a short one, but the depth of feeling in her welcome had thrown him off balance.

"Shall we start walking?" he said. "It's cold hanging about."

He wanted to ask them about Robert's death, but he was afraid of a new rush of embarrassing emotion, and they walked in silence. They walked down the track and had almost reached the road by the time Alec met them.

Maggie was the first customer in the hall. She had come out to escape from Buness. The conversation with George and Sarah had worried her more than she would admit to herself and she felt unwell, with a piercing headache above one eye. At home she had felt restless and trapped. She was confused by this. Usually the house gave her power. It was her domain and she loved being there. Without the house and her role in the family she had no importance. She felt her confidence crumbling. She wondered what Alec was doing. He had been in a foul temper since coming home the afternoon before. She had asked him if he had seen George. Alec had sworn at her and accused her of sending folk to spy on him. She had wanted to discuss things calmly, so that at least they could agree on what they should say if there were any more questions, but he had refused to talk to her. She had remained silent at breakfast, because the boys were there, and immediately afterwards Alec had gone out without telling her how he was planning to spend the day. She was used to Alec's bouts of childish temper and usually ignored them as she did her children's tantrums, but now she wondered if his present mood had a more sinister significance.

At the sale she was a discriminating customer. She hunted through a pile of clothes for a real bargain, checking every seam and hem, feeling the quality of the cloth between thumb and fingers. She realized, as she held the cheap cloth to her cheek, that she was frightened.

James heard the plane and at Melissa's insistence he telephoned Kenneth Dance to find out who had arrived on the island.

"It's the Woollie Man," he said, expecting her not to be interested. He had gone to the sale in the past, but she had not seemed to like the things he had chosen to bring home for her.

"Shall we go?" she asked. He was astounded. Usually a panic attack affected her for weeks. But since George Palmer-Jones had left them alone she seemed altogether stronger, more determined. It was as if she had something to fight for.

"Shall we go?" she repeated. "I would like to."

"Are you sure?"

"Yes. We'll show them."

He did not understand. He was pleased by the change in her, but it worried him, too. It was all too sudden. Everyone on Kinness was frightened of change.

"We'll go, then," he said, "but if you want to leave the hall, you must say."

"I won't show you up."

He could not remember the last time they had walked out together, arm in arm in the sunshine. He felt that it should have been a

Sunday. Kinness couples often walked out like that on Sunday afternoons when he and Melissa had stayed in the house. He supposed that there was work he should be doing in the croft, but this was more important. He could feel her body close to his as they walked. With every step she swayed against him and the sharp bone of her hip touched his leg. The closeness made him feel breathless, like a young boy out with a girl for the first time.

When they approached the hall, her arm tightened on his, but she did not hesitate.

"Are you all right?"

"Yes."

"We'll go in then?"

"Yes."

He held the door open and she walked ahead of him into the hall. Her back was very straight. People turned towards her, smiling. She smiled and smiled all morning and thought how clever she was to keep it up. Because she knew that she had nothing to smile about.

Elspeth did not want to go to the sale, but her parents persuaded her.

"There'll be nothing worth buying there," she said, knowing that it was only an excuse.

"If you're staying on here for a while, Ben will need more things for school," her mother said. "Hard-wearing things. Island wool's good for Sunday best but it doesn't wear well."

"Do you want me out, then?" Elspeth knew that she was overreacting. She wanted to cry. "I know that you're ashamed of me, too."

"That's foolish," her father said gently. "You stay until you want to go. We want you here."

"You want to keep an eye on me. You don't trust me."

"That's foolish," he said. He and Annie shared the conspiratorial, slightly superior look of doctors coming to a decision about a difficult patient, which Elspeth recognized and resented. "There's no point opening the shop this morning. Everyone will be in the hall. We'll all go."

So she agreed to go with them, because if she had refused she would have been thought neurotic and ungrateful. They hardly let her out of their sight now. She longed to be alone. She had hoped that her time on the island would bring a kind of peace. She found it occasionally when lying on the short grass at the top of the cliffs watching the seabirds. She was drawn to the cliffs, and never spent as much time there as she would have liked. Her parents filled her day with chores and visits and she had little time to herself.

Sometimes she wished that everything were out in the open. Then, at least, they would allow her to be alone. But she felt unable to take the active step of telling anyone about Gordon. She justified her silence by pretending that it was to protect Ben and her parents, but she knew that not to be true. She had never taken any active step in organizing her life. She drifted, like a fulmar hanging on the currents just below the cliff edge, and left everything to fate.

Jim told Sarah about the Woollie Man when he came in for breakfast. She laughed.

"Isn't bringing jumpers to Kinness like selling coals to Newcastle?" she asked.

"You'll not want to go, then?" He was a little surprised. All the island women looked forward to the sale.

"I don't suppose I'll buy anything, but I'll go along."

She did not like to admit it to herself, but the thought of a day at home bored her. She had become used to the drama of George's investigation. She looked at Jim—at the square, uncomplicated face and the square rugby-player's body—and wondered, horribly, if she would ever be bored with him.

"What else will you do today?" he asked.

She was surprised by the question.

"What do you mean?"

"Are you going out with George again?"

"I hadn't planned to. Would you mind?"

He considered.

"It doesn't make it any easier for me," he said. "Alec was going on about it this morning."

"What did you say to him?"

"I said that it was your business and I trusted you to do what was right."

"Did you?" She was pleased by his answer but somehow daunted by it. Her decision to go with George had been unthinking, frivolous, and he made it sound so serious. "I'm sorry," she went on. "It can't be easy for you. Do you want me to stop? I'm not really involved. I don't know why George was so keen to have me there."

He thought about it, looked at her. He never makes any decision on impulse, she thought. Everything's carefully considered. Then she thought that he had been romantic and impulsive in his love for Elspeth, and she disliked Elspeth for having changed him, robbed him of spontaneity.

"I meant what I said." He stood up, prepared to go out again. "I do trust you. Carry on if you feel you have to."

George Palmer-Jones had no intention of going to the sale until Alec's car drove past the school house and he saw Will's moody, teenage face at the car window. Will had been living at Sandwick when Mary had died. He was closest to her in age. Perhaps she had confided in him. Perhaps he knew her secret. The children were out to play and he walked round to the school room to tell Jonathan Drysdale where he was going.

"It's like a glorified jumble sale," Jonathan said. "Everything he has to sell is trash. But they'll all be there convinced that they've got a bargain."

"I think I'll go and see what's going on. I might buy you a present."

Drysdale was not amused. He went into the playground and rang the school bell with a bitter ferocity.

Will sat outside the hall, on the grass, leaning against the outside wall of the graveyard. He knew that it was a churlish and ineffective gesture to refuse to go into the sale, but he felt manipulated and frustrated. It was quite clear that his mother expected him to live on the island forever. He would have to tell her that it was impossible, and there would be a scene. He felt, too, that some important information was being kept from him. Robert's death had not been mentioned, and when they spoke of Mary it was with anger. They expected so much of him, but gave very little in return. He was wearing binoculars and began to look at the skylarks at the edge of the stubble field below him. For a while he forgot his family and became absorbed in watching the birds in the sharp, clear light. He stared at a smaller, more compact bird which attracted then held his attention.

He was still there when George came along. George had only seen him a few times on previous visits to the islands, but the common interest in natural history was strong enough to allow the sort of easy conversation which usually comes with friendship. The boy heard him approaching, looked up, and smiled.

"I think I've just seen a short-toed lark," he said. "I was wondering if I should go up to the school and tell Jonathan. He might want to see it in his lunch break."

"No, don't go," George said quickly. "I'll tell Jonathan when I go back."

They watched the bird together. George confirmed the identification, then there was a relaxed and friendly silence.

"Why did you decide to come home?" George asked.

"I didn't decide. It was decided for me." Will put down his binoculars. "What's going on here?" The question came out in desperation.

"Did your mother tell you about Robert?"

"She said that he had died. In a shooting accident."

"I don't think the police even believe that it was an accident. He was murdered. Like Mary."

"Mary fell over the cliff."

"She was pushed."

George thought that Will was going to cry. It was all too much for him to take in. His arrogance had disappeared and he seemed very young.

"Why didn't they tell me?" Will said. He was angry and upset. "Why did they hide it from me?"

"I'm the only person who is certain that it was murder."

"Who did it?"

"I don't know yet. I need your help. Mary had a secret. She knew something about someone on the island which would have caused so much embarrassment that she had to be prevented from telling it. I believe that Robert found out about it, too, so he had to die."

"No," Will said. "It can't have happened like that."

"Tell me why?"

Will struggled to find the words to explain. "What matters is appearance. The whole island might know of something going on, but as long as no one admits that they know, life can continue as usual. It's the only way, I suppose, that people have managed to live on top of each other for all these years."

"But if Mary were to discover a secret like that, she would make a fuss about it. No one would be able to pretend, then, that they didn't know."

"But you don't understand," Will cried. "The secret probably wasn't terrible at all. It was probably a little thing. Certainly nothing to commit murder for. It might be a major scandal here if the teacher refuses to go to church or someone kisses someone else's wife after having too much to drink on Friday night, but it's not a matter of murder."

George spoke quietly.

"You believe you know Mary's secret, don't you?"

"Yes."

He put his head in his hands.

"Is it about Sylvia Drysdale and Alec?"

"How did you know?" The boy felt cheated of the drama of revelation. He was surprised and annoyed.

"As you said, it wasn't a very well-kept secret. But no one else is prepared to talk about it. Can you tell me, in confidence, what was going on between Sylvia and Alec, and what the island, especially Maggie and Jonathan, thought about it?"

"What does it have to do with you?" Will had recovered his poise, adopted again the pose of cool experience.

"Does it matter? Do you want to protect a murderer?" The words were sharp and Will had no defence against them.

"I'll tell you," he said, trying to pretend that the decision to speak was his. "It won't do any good but I'll tell you. Do you want to go somewhere more private?"

George looked towards the hall. The people coming and going directed their attention to each other, and the goods for sale, and the turbaned Woollie Man. If anyone saw them, it would be assumed that they were birdwatching.

"No. This will do. When did it all start?"

"I don't know exactly. Of course I was out at school until July. There was a big picnic the first fine weekend we were home—there always is—and then a dance afterwards. I didn't notice anything. Sylvia looked lovely, but she always does. The women here say that she shows off, but it's the way she is. She danced a lot with Alec, but they're both fine dancers and they enjoy dancing together. She danced with other men, too. Maggie left early to put the boys to bed and later all the family came back to Sandwick for coffee and a dram. Alec wasn't there at first and we thought he'd gone straight home to Buness. Then he came in. He was very drunk and seemed pleased with himself, boastful. You can never tell how much is true with him, and how much is wishful thinking, but he said that he'd just walked Sylvia Drysdale home. He started telling us what had happened when he saw that Uncle James was in the room and he shut up. Uncle James is the lay preacher."

"I know," George said. "What exactly did he say before he saw James?"

"He said that she was a good screw." He blushed, and became a child again. "It probably never happened. He tells terrible stories."

George ignored his embarrassment. "What happened next?" he asked.

"I don't think very much happened. He hung around her all summer. He was always trying to find excuses to get her on her own, but it's not easy on a place as small as this, and he just made a fool of himself. I don't think she was really interested. She liked the admiration but she didn't take him seriously. You can't blame her. She was used to a more exciting life than this."

"You mean that all this fuss has been over one incident three months ago?"

"As far as I know. Since then Sylvia's been flirting with Alec just to annoy Maggie."

"How has Maggie reacted to it?"

"At first she just ignored him. She thought he was all talk and no action. It's happened before. He's disappeared up to Ellie's Head after a dance with a pretty young woman several times, but they've always been visitors to the island, so it never mattered so much. More recently I think all the gossip has been getting her down."

"And Jonathan? Was he similarly tolerant?"

"He seemed to be. He knows that Sylvia isn't happy here."

George was disappointed. He had expected there to be something more. A real motive for murder. But he showed no disappointment.

"Did you notice when Mary left the hall on the night of the party?" he asked.

"No. I was playing guitar for the band. She wasn't around in the interval."

"What did you do in the interval?"

"I had a drink and something to eat."

George could remember seeing him, lounging against the wall, watching the rest of the crowd with a detached, rather superior air.

"Did you notice if anyone was away for a long time before or during the interval?"

"No. I didn't notice."

No, George thought, you were busy wondering what people were thinking of you.

They sat in silence again watching the short-toed lark in the field. Each spike of stubble was hard and clear in the sunshine. All the colours on the bird were very bright. The hall was full now. There was no one else outside and it was very quiet.

"It must be something else," George said, almost to himself. "There must be another secret. You don't know what it can be?"

"No."

Suddenly, from inside the hall, there was the sound of a scream. It was of anger and exasperation, not of pain, but it was loud enough to make the short-toed lark rise into the air before settling again farther away. Elspeth ran out of the hall towards them. Tears were streaming down her face and she took no notice of the men. She was completely absorbed in her own misery. She was wearing a calf-length skirt, and as she ran she stumbled and caught her knee on the hem. Will called after her but she took no notice. When she reached the road, he got up and hurried after her without saying a word to George.

George walked slowly towards the hall. As he reached the door Kenneth and Annie came out. Annie, too, looked as if she had been crying. Kenneth had his arm around her shoulder. They followed their daughter home, like grieving relatives following a coffin at a funeral.

Obviously everyone inside the hall had enjoyed the disturbance, yet they were shocked by it. The scene was another indication that everything was not as normal. The clothes for sale on the trestles were ignored and people stood in small groups, talking. Some of the wedding decorations were still strung over the ceiling, and with the colourful clothes, the place still had a fantastic carnival air. When George walked in, the islanders stared at him, hoping that he might have the power to satisfy their curiosity, but he took no notice and they turned back to their friends to gossip and speculate. The Woollie Man held up some violently striped towels in a last effort to attract custom, but there was no response, and he began to pile the unsold goods into suitcases.

Sarah was there, talking to Agnes, and George approached her. "What was that about?" he asked.

"It was really strange.. .." Her voice was clear and piercing and people turned to look at her, waiting for her interpretation of the incident which had taken place.

He took her arm and led her outside. The audience was hostile, resentful because they were being deprived of another free show. Sarah seemed not to notice them. She seemed as excited as all the others. Once outside she continued:

"It was really strange. Elspeth went up to the counter to buy some things for her little boy. The salesman was talking to her, joking, you know, saying how pretty she was. Then when he was giving her the change, he said he thought he recognized her and hadn't she been on the television? She said no, of course she hadn't. You could tell that she was hating it. She was almost shouting. But he insisted. He said he had a wonderful memory and he was sure he'd seen her face on the television. That was when she screamed and ran out.

"The funny thing was that I looked at Annie while it was going on and she was upset too."

"The salesman wasn't specific? He didn't say how long ago he'd seen her or what sort of programme it was?"

She shook her head.

"No. It happened just as I told you."

He waited until she had walked away before he went back into the hall to talk to the Woollie Man. All the customers had gone and the trestle tables were empty. A shaft of sunlight came in through the open door and showed the dust in the air and the cobwebs on the rafters. The Woollie Man answered his questions with a polite bewilderment, but he provided no more useful information. He was very sorry that he had upset the young lady. He had not meant to do that. He thought that she must be famous because he had seen her face on the television. Once a famous actress had bought from his stall in Glasgow.

"Are you based in Glasgow?"

"Yes, I travel. It's six months since I was there, but Glasgow is my home."

"The young lady comes from Glasgow. Perhaps you met her there."

"Perhaps."

He was no longer interested. He had not sold as much as he

had expected and he was disappointed. He wanted to finish clearing away.

George was at the door when he turned back.

"I wonder," he said. "Could I come out with you on the plane? I'd pay half of the charter cost."

The man grinned.

"Sure," he said. "Sure."

At the school the children were out to play for lunchtime. The girls had a skipping rope and were singing a rhyme. The boys were playing spacemen. Ben Dance sat on a wall and watched the children, but made no attempt to join in.

Jonathan sat at his desk in the school room drinking a mug of coffee. He was reading the manuscript of a paper about gull population control sent by an ornithological magazine for his comments. He was concentrating so hard that he did not hear George come in.

"There's a short-toed lark on the stubble field below the hall," George said.

"That's good. I'll get down to see it after school."

"Will Stennet found it."

"Is he back? I'll have to arrange the swan-ringing expedition, then."

"I'm going out on the plane. I'll stay on Baltasay tonight and come back on the *Ruth Isabella* tomorrow."

"Will you see Sylvia?"

"Probably. But that's not why I'm going."

"Tell her that I miss her," Jonathan said abruptly, "and that I'll leave the island as soon as I can get another job. Before that if she's desperate to go."

"I'll tell her."

"The police phoned from Baltasay," Jonathan said, "just after you'd gone out. They're coming in this afternoon, in their own plane."

"They'll miss me, then."

He went into the house to pack an overnight bag, then began to walk to the airstrip. He hoped to leave before the police arrived on Kinness. It was not that he felt in competition with them. He would have been glad of a chance to discuss the information that Elspeth Dance had a secret and was frightened of being recognized. But he knew that they would not be interested. They were willing to consider that Robert's death was murder, but he was certain that Robert had died only because he shared Mary Stennet's knowledge. Mary Stennet's death was the key to the thing, and they believed that she was a foolhardy girl who had slipped.

He enjoyed the walk to the airstrip and got there before Alec's car or the aeroplane. He heard the engine of the plane first, then Alec's car raced up the track and stopped dramatically with squealing brakes and a cloud of sand, just as the plane touched down.

As the Woollie Man unloaded his luggage from the boot, Alec stuck his head through the car window and shouted at George:

"You're leaving then, are you? You rake up all the muck and then you piss off. Well, don't think you'll be welcome on Kinness again."

Perhaps he thought that George would not hear him. The noise of the plane's engine was very loud. George got in and chose a seat by the window. The plane took off and circled the island once before heading for Baltasay. George looked at Kinness, green and perfect below him, and he knew that what Alec had said was true. However things turned out, he would never be welcome on the island again, and once the matter was resolved, he knew he would never return.

Chapter Eleven

That afternoon Sarah met Elspeth quite by chance. Alec had told her that George had gone to Baltasay. She supposed that he was following some line of investigation and felt resentful because he had not told her why he was going. Jim had refused her offer of help on the croft and she did not want to stay inside. The sunshine tempted her to explore.

On the west side of the island there was a small, sandy beach. Sarah saw it from the clifftop and thought that she could get down to it. It was an adventure. When she got to the beach, Elspeth was already there. Sarah had not seen her from the clifftop. She was sitting on a rock and she was crying. She was wearing a shawl round her shoulders and Sarah thought that the first Ellie Dance must have looked like that. Sarah did not know what to do. Elspeth had not seen her, she was staring out to sea with a mournful, melodramatic air. Then Sarah slipped on the shingle at the top of the beach. The pebbles rattled and bounced with a sound like gunshot and Elspeth turned and saw her.

"I'm sorry," Sarah said awkwardly, walking up to the rock. "I didn't know you were here. I didn't mean to disturb you."

"I suppose that they're all talking about me," Elspeth said, "because I made a fool of myself at the sale." She had not dried her tears and her face was red and blotchy like a miserable child's. "I suppose I should be used to it by now, but the thought of all the tongues wagging still bothers me."

She seemed not to expect any answer and continued:

"The police are coming in this afternoon to ask more questions about Robert. I wish they'd stop. I hate it."

With another sudden change of conversation she said:

"You seem very happy with Jim. I've been jealous. I suppose I'm a bitch."

"It must have been difficult," Sarah said carefully. "All the fuss about the wedding. If you still cared for Jim."

"Yes. It was difficult. It wouldn't have worked, if we'd married. He would have hated me very soon. But it was nice to dream about. I suppose we all need something to dream about during the difficult times. I dreamt about coming home and marrying Jim. When I got here, I found that he was already engaged to a pretty English girl."

"But you didn't pin the note on my wedding dress?"

"No." She did not ask for an explanation for the question. "I hoped that you wouldn't like it here," she said. "I hoped that you would leave. But it must have been horrible. First Mary and now Robert."

"It hasn't been too comfortable."

"I wonder if I would have been different, nicer, if I'd been born somewhere else," Elspeth said. "I seem to have been doomed from birth. I was named after a girl who went mad and committed suicide."

"I know."

"It haunts me sometimes. As if that's my fate, too, and there's nothing I can do to prevent it."

"That's ridiculous. And it's an excuse for making no effort to determine your own future."

"Perhaps. But that's how I feel. I tried to explain to them in Glasgow but they couldn't understand. They thought I was making excuses."

"There's Ben," Sarah said. "You have to make a future for him."

"They said that in Glasgow too. And they were right. Of course they were right. But they didn't know how guilty I felt, and that it helped sometimes to think that I wasn't entirely responsible."

"Elspeth," Sarah said, "what happened in Glasgow?"

She was quite sure that Elspeth was preparing to tell her everything. She felt very close to the other woman. She could smell the wet wool of the shawl mixed with the odour of salt and seaweed. Sheltered by the cliffs, they could see nothing of the island, and the middle-aged gossips in the tidy white houses seemed a thousand miles away.

Then around the bottom of the cliff, looking out of place in his working clothes, walked Kenneth Dance. He was wearing Wellingtons over his grey trousers, but the tie, the neat waistcoat, and grey jacket made it seem that he had left the post office in a hurry. He was obviously finding the exertion of the walk uncomfortable, and stopped to catch his breath.

"Damn that man," Elspeth said. "He's spying on me. He follows me everywhere."

"He can't hear us."

"It's no good. He doesn't trust me. He's come to take me home to face the police."

Sarah expected her to walk down the beach towards her father, but she ran away up the cliff, her shoes in her hand and the shawl in a tangled mat around her shoulders. Kenneth Dance looked helplessly as she disappeared, then walked back the way he had come.

As he went the plane flew in again.

George was surprised to find Sylvia waiting for him at the Baltasay airport in a hire car.

"Jonathan telephoned me and said you were coming." she said, "I thought this would save you the bother of coming to find me."

"It was kind of you."

"Oh, I've been starting to feel bored again. Baltasay isn't very much more entertaining than Kinness."

She turned to him and smiled and he felt that she was pleased to see him.

"Where do you want to go?" she asked.

"Would you mind if we had tea? I missed lunch. Perhaps we could have a proper island tea with scones and cakes."

She laughed, and as she tipped back her head her long earrings moved and reflected the warm colour of her skin. He was glad to be alone with her.

She took him to the hotel where James had courted Melissa. It had not changed very much. They sat in a large, gloomy lounge, surrounded by dark stained wood. They were alone.

"Why have you come?" she asked. "There's no mystery about my leaving, and I'm going back to Kinness on the next boat. Won't your questions wait until then?"

She was humouring him, taking an interest in the inquiry through politeness. She thought that he was bored, as she was, missing his work, and he had to create a little diversion for himself, to pass the time.

"They would have waited," he said. "Something else brought me to Baltasay."

"Did it?" Again she was not really interested. She was pouring the tea and she seemed to be devoting her attention to giving him just the right amount of milk. But he felt that her thoughts were elsewhere. It was not that she was anxious, only preoccupied with a pleasant daydream. She looked up and saw that he was watching her.

"I'm sorry that I left the island in such an impulsive way. Did you think that I was your murderer?"

She realized that she had gone too far. He knew that she was mocking him. "I'm sorry," she said again. "What do you want to know?"

"I want to know your secret."

She had not expected this and gave him her full attention. The languorous mood was over.

"That's very ungallant," she said, recovering herself. "No woman will reveal all her secrets."

"Start by telling me about Alec Stennet."

She was relieved and laughed again. She stretched a long, smooth arm across the polished table, then turned the palm of the hand up in a gesture of indifference.

"One night at a party he got drunk and I let him walk home with me. Jonathan had left hours before. He's an unsocial bore at times. I must have been drunk, too, because I let Alec kiss me. He is handsome, you know, in a strange, brutish way. He won't let me forget it and neither will the island. It was only a kiss, despite what he's told them. They think I'm a scarlet woman anyway because I won't go to church, so they're quite prepared to think the worst of me. There would hardly be less gossip if I were running a brothel in the school house. Alec's attentions were entertaining for a while, but they became tedious."

Her diversion, he thought, her relief from boredom.

"And there are no other secrets?" he asked.

"Nothing that I'd be prepared to talk to you about." She smiled. "And nothing that could have any relevance to Mary's death."

"Jonathan did tell you," George said slowly, "that Robert was murdered?"

"No." She was very shocked. "He said there was an accident with a shotgun."

"It was murder," George said. "The police are back on Kinness this afternoon, asking questions." He paused. "I shall have to tell them that Robert was on the hill on Monday morning, watching you. You were in the empty croft, talking to someone."

"No." Her hands were shaking and she lit a cigarette. "I told you at the time. I was on my own."

"You should tell me. It may have no relevance."

"No."

As she sat and smoked she seemed to recover her poise. Despite her refusal to answer his questions George knew that he wanted to prolong the encounter. It was as if she had enchanted him, and he were unable to let her go.

"I have a message for you," he said, "from Jonathan."

She waited with polite but wary interest. She was turning the wedding ring round and round on her finger, but gave no other sign of concern.

"He says that he will leave the island as soon as he can get another job. Before that if it makes you happy."

There was no reaction.

"Does he?" she said. "I think, you know, that it's a little late for that."

She was staying at the hotel and excused herself to go upstairs to prepare to go out. She had arranged to meet a friend, a woman she stressed, who taught music at the high school. There was an exhibition of local art in the museum and they were going together. He watched her walk across the lounge, then poured himself another cup of tea from the ample pot. He seemed unable to leave. He was tied to her.

She was away for longer than he had expected, and he felt foolish, sitting by the dirty plates in the empty room. When she came down the stairs at last, she was dressed in a warm jacket and leather boots. She saw him through the open door of the lounge, but she did not approach him again. She waved and went out. He had the impression that she was running away from him.

He waited until she left the building, then walked to the reception desk. The receptionist was a local girl, buxom and saucy, with a round red face. She grinned at him.

"It's very quiet here today," he said.

"You're telling me. I've not spoken to a soul since lunchtime." It was a great hardship to her, this solitude.

"As it's so quiet, I suppose you'd remember all the incoming telephone calls received by your guests."

"I might." She was curious but suspicious.

"I'm a private detective," he said confidentially. "It's a divorce matter."

She was enthralled. "You want to know about the lady you were taking tea with?" She had no hesitation now in talking to him.

"Yes. Has she had any telephone calls since she's been staying here?"

"I'm not here all the time, of course." She spoke in a stage whisper, although there was no one to hear. "I was working last night and there were two calls for her then."

"Did you take the calls yourself?"

"Yes I did."

"Do you remember anything about them? Were the callers men or women?"

"They were both men."

"It wasn't the same man ringing twice?"

"Certainly not." She was indignant that he should question her competence at information-gathering. She was obviously skilled at it. It was her way of passing the time. "The voices were quite different."

"In what way?"

"One was la-di-da. Toffee-nosed English. A bit like the lady speaks. The other was local, an islander. Not from Baltasay, though. From one of the outer isles. I'd say he came from Kinness."

"Would you?" He nodded. "I see."

"Is that useful?" she asked excitedly.

"Oh yes. Very useful."

She was thrilled to have helped him.

After he had left the hotel he wondered if he should have paid her for the information. It had not occurred to him. He thought she would feel that she had been adequately rewarded because her afternoon would pass much more quickly and she would have something to chat about to her friends.

What had he learnt? The toffee-nosed Englishman was obviously Jonathan, but who was the other man with the Kinness accent? Perhaps Alec refused to accept that Sylvia was no longer interested in him. That was possible. She was very attractive.

He walked along the quay past the fishing boats, the big oil supply vessels. The town was busy. Children, just out of school, lingered around the harbour, putting off the time of parents and homework. The move to the high school must be hard for the Kinness children, George thought. They had to face the sudden exposure to the bustle and relative anonymity of the small town without the support of their parents. Did they revel in the freedom or were they dreadfully homesick? He remembered Will's resentment at being dragged back to Kinness. He at least had been happy to leave the island. Wouldn't everything have been different if Mary had been allowed out to Baltasay, too? She would have had friends of her own age. More stimulating school work. There would have been more to think about than adult secrets.

George walked to the telephone box by the ferry office and phoned the library to find out whether it would still be open that evening. He had, after all, come to Baltasay to use the library, but it was in the same building as the museum and he preferred to wait until Sylvia had finished her visit to the art exhibition before he went there. He did not want her to see him. A soft-spoken, elderly lady told him the library would be open until eight.

He supposed that he should find somewhere to stay. He could spend the night in the hotel, and he imagined for a moment walking into the restaurant with Sylvia on his arm. It was a pleasant image, but he put it from his mind. He needed to be alone. At random he chose one of the cottages by the harbour, which had a bed and breakfast sign in the garden. A big woman with a flowered overall opened the door to him and showed him into a small square room with a window looking out to sea. The bed was old and high and had hard white sheets. He smiled his acceptance of the room. She relaxed, offered him tea, and when he refused, began a lengthy conversation.

"Would you like supper, then? I'll be cooking for Jerry, my husband. It'll be nothing special, but you could have a meal if you wanted. At about half past six . . ."

It turned out that Jerry worked on his father's fishing boat. George enjoyed listening to the details of the fishing trips and her domestic life but he began to wonder, after a quarter of an hour, how he could tell her tactfully that he wanted to be alone. Then two children came through the back gate below him, their satchels heavy on their shoulders, knees and shoes scuffed with playground games, and she went downstairs to make hot, sweet tea for them and to cut lumps of sticky flapjack to keep them going to supper.

George sat on the bed, looked out over the sea, and considered the information he had gained that day. He had known for some time that Elspeth was hiding something. She was so tense, so reluctant to discuss her past, and her parents were too protective. Of course she had been recently divorced, but there was something else, too, and her peculiar reaction to the Sikh salesman proved it. Now he had a clue to her secret, and there was a possibility that he could discover what it was. The Woollie Man said that she had been on television. If she had taken part in a chat show or quiz show, there would have been no reason not to admit it. It must, George thought, have been a news item. Nothing else would have provoked that reaction. More specifically she must have been featured on a local news programme. If she was part of national news coverage, the people on Kinness would have seen it. But how can it be relevant anyway? he thought. If Elspeth had managed to keep her secret from the rest of Kinness, surely Mary would never have been able to find it out.

His thoughts returned to Sylvia and her intense shock at learning that Robert had been murdered. Perhaps her secret was more important, and the trip to Baltasay was a wild-goose chase.

Then with a sudden panic he wondered if he had got it all wrong, and if Mary's talk of a secret was just misleading. There were other tensions on the island. The hostility between the Stennets and Dances smouldered as it had done for generations. There was pressure on land and space. He knew that he was obsessed by Mary's secret and that the obsession was caused by guilt, because he had not persuaded her to share it.

It was dark. The tide was high and the lights from the town and the boats reflected in the water. He had been on Kinness long enough for the electricity to appear magical. There was a knock on the door. It was opened by one of the landlady's sons.

"Mum says that dinner's ready," the boy said, and he could hardly keep the amusement from his voice because the old man looked so funny sitting there in the dark.

George went to the bathroom to wash his hands, then went downstairs to eat.

He would have welcomed the company of the family—he could hear them talking and laughing in the kitchen to the background of television commercials—but his landlady had laid a table in the dining room for him and he ate alone. So even as he enjoyed the food, theories about the case persisted, and he could not forget it.

His landlady saw him out.

"We don't lock the door," she said. "I'll make you a cup of tea when you come in."

He walked down the high street towards the library. There were small groups of men talking and laughing. Noise and warmth and men spilled out on to the pavement from a busy bar. He envied the companionable warmth of the people leaning against the bar, and was so convinced that the trip to the library was doomed to failure that he almost gave up and joined them. Why should a library on Baltasay keep copies of mainland papers which were six months old? When he was on Kinness and the Woollie Man with his pedlar's suitcases and his aeroplane offered the promise of escape, it had seemed quite reasonable. Now the idea was ludicrous. But he walked past the open door of the bar. He was here now and he had to try.

The library was a new building, bought with a grant from an oil company. It was brightly lit, very peaceful, nearly empty. The elderly woman to whom he had spoken on the telephone sat behind the desk. She listened carefully to his request, but as he had expected she could not help him.

"We keep copies of the local paper," she said, "for the museum. You'd be welcome to look at those." Her voice was so soft that it seemed hardly to be human. "We take the national dailies of course, but we don't keep them, not for more than a week."

He said that he would look throuh copies of the weekly local paper, starting three months before and working back, but he knew that it would be no good. The *Baltasay Times* was a week old by the time it reached Kinness, but everyone took it. If there were any mention of Elspeth in the paper, it would have been noticed and talked about. He needed one of the Scottish papers, based in Glasgow.

The librarian brought the files of the newspaper to him and he sat at a round pine table to read them. The artificial light and the background hum of the central heating reminded him of the office where he had worked before his retirement. The newspapers were a fascinating record of island life and he would have enjoyed giving them more attention, but they contained nothing which interested him.

He took the newspapers back to the desk and the little woman must have sensed his disappointment.

"You don't want to go further back?" she asked.

He shook his head. He had read copies back to the beginning of the year. For Elspeth's face to have lodged in the Woollie Man's memory she must have been on the television very soon before he began his sales tour of the Northern Isles. That, too, would have fitted in with Elspeth's arrival on Kinness.

It was quarter to eight. It seemed unlikely that there would be more visitors to the library. George felt sleepy, resigned to failure, but he was enjoying the comforting, familiar warmth of the building. Perhaps the librarian wished that he would go so that she could close and have an early night, but she had gone to the trouble of gathering together that week's national papers for him to look at. He had missed seeing a newspaper on Kinness—no one bothered taking a daily there—so he sat back at his table and prepared to read them.

Elspeth's face stared out at him immediately and he was astounded. The paper was only four days old. She was on Kinness then. How could she be making news? He looked back at the paper, afraid that he might be mistaken, but it was certainly Elspeth, staring straight at the camera, her hair dragged from her face.

It was the Scottish edition of a daily paper. The headline above the photograph read: CHILD ATTACKER NOT TO BE RELEASED. The article was a report of an appeal judgment. Gordon Bain had been sentenced to five years' imprisonment in the previous March for ill treating his son. He had appealed against his sentence and the article reported that the appeal had been dismissed. The newspaper seemed to have run a campaign after the original case, calling for an inquiry, and had interviewed doctors, social workers, and teachers at the time of the trial. Now it was using the appeal to renew the campaign.

It was at this point that Elspeth was mentioned. "Mr. Bain's wife Elspeth was found not guilty in March of assaulting her child. It was said by a psychiatrist for her defence that she had no recognized mental illness but that she was under her husband's domination. However, it was admitted that she did nothing to prevent Mr. Bain inflicting horrific injuries to the boy. It was only when a violent blow to the head rendered six-year-old Ben unconscious that she took him to the hospital casualty department and revealed what had been happening. We find it most disturbing that on his discharge from hospital little Ben was returned to his mother's care. We contacted the social services department today to ask what steps were being taken to supervise Mrs. Bain's care of her child. We were given no adequate reply."

Once he knew, the thing become obvious. He remembered the boy, Ben, the white, worried, old-man's face, the old-fashioned deference when he spoke to adults. Molly always said that battered children were unnaturally polite and well behaved. No wonder that Kenneth and Annie had made every effort to protect Elspeth, to prevent her secret from becoming public knowledge. The stigma of being involved in a court case was bad enough, but this was a hundred times worse. Families and children were very important on Kinness.

It occurred to him then that Will must have known what Elspeth had been going through. George remembered that he and Will had been sitting together outside the hall when Elspeth had run out of the Woollie Man's sale in such distress and that Will had followed her. Will would have been on Baltasay during the trial and may have seen a report of it there. He hoped that Elspeth had been able to talk to Will. She needed to confide in somebody.

It was eight o'clock and the librarian hovered beside his table. She wanted to go home, but she did not want to seem to hurry him. He handed the newspapers to her, but the words of the article remained with him.

"Were they any help?" she asked hopefully.

"Oh yes," he said politely. "Very helpful."

She walked with him to the door and saw him out into the street. How could she do it? he thought, seeing again the white face of the boy and the photograph of the woman in the paper, her hair pulled back, her face naked and exposed to the camera. How could she allow her child to be maltreated? The angry adjectives of the gutter press returned to him—she's evil, wicked, he thought. Molly would have said that it was wrong to judge. He did not know all the facts. He wished that Molly was with him to explain.

He walked down the high street to the bar he had passed. Inside it was noisy and rough. It made no pretence than to be other than a place to drink. It suited him. He stood at the bar and drank one large scotch after another until closing time. Then, as straight as a sergeant major, he walked back to his landlady's cottage. He opened the door quietly, and by the time his landlady heard his footsteps on the stairs and came from the kitchen to offer him tea, he was in his own room.

Chapter Twelve

George woke the next morning with the image of Elspeth's face. He had drunk himself to sleep but he could not forget it. There were household sounds—a grate being riddled, pans, a gurgling cistern. He got up. The weather had changed. There was low cloud and drizzle and he could not see the harbour.

Downstairs the landlady was surprised that he was up so early. He accepted tea from her, but no breakfast, paid her, and left.

The police station was a square building of grey stone near to the quay. It would have been the harbourmaster's office or a chandlery. It was like all the other square grey houses in the street. At the desk a policeman was reading a newspaper and seemed surprised to see him, too.

"I'd like to see Inspector Johnson," George said, naming the officer who had come to Kinness.

The constable took his name and asked him to wait. He returned almost immediately and showed George up some stone stairs and into an office.

Johnson stood up and held out his hand. He was clearly ill at ease and embarrassed.

"It's good of you to come in to see me, sir," he said. "We missed you on Kinness yesterday."

He motioned to George to sit down. The next words came out all together.

"I hope I didn't seem rude when we met on the island," he said. "I didn't know who you were then, you see. I read your textbook on interviewing techniques when I was at training school. Very useful I found it."

George ignored the flattery. He wanted to say that the fact that he had once worked for the Home Office should make no difference. The policemen had known the facts and should have made a sensible and logical reconstruction of events. It's a pity you didn't take more notice of my chapter on "listening to witnesses," he wanted to say. But that would not have been constructive.

"As you seem to have been checking the background of your suspects," he said, "you'll know about Elspeth Dance."

"Yes." The policeman looked awkward. "She was charged with battering her child last spring and found not guilty. But that was quite a different sort of case. I don't see how it can be relevant to this."

"A child was involved." George was almost shrieking. That similarity must be obvious even to the police on Baltasay, who had to deal with nothing more complicated than drunken brawls on a Friday night. "And no one from Kinness knew that she had been in court. I explained to you about Mary Stennet's secret. Don't you see that must make Elspeth Dance a suspect?"

"I know you're very involved with the case, sir," Johnson said, "but I've been discussing it with the super-intendent and we still don't think these are grounds to consider that the young girl's death was murder. He thinks it more likely that the old man was involved in a bit of an argument, someone lost their temper. It happens quite often in the outlying islands. Nothing more complicated than that."

I was right, George thought, they're not prepared to consider anything other than a drunken brawl. It's all that they're used to.

He tried to control his temper.

"You do accept, then," he said quietly, "that Robert was murdered?"

"No doubt about it," said the policeman, glad to return to a point on which they would agree. "The gun was fired only a few yards from the victim. There's no way that it could have been an accident. I doubt if we'll ever find out who did it. They're a close lot on the outer islands. I expect they all know who it was, but no one's prepared to talk."

"I won't take up any more of your time, Inspector," George said. He felt the weight of responsibility. It was as if the police had given up, and had handed over the task of finding the murderer to him. He stood up and left the room.

Sylvia Drysdale had arrived at Lutwick before him. She must have hired a taxi, too. It would have been sensible, he supposed, to share one, but he had wanted to be alone. She stood, looking out to sea, watching for the first glimpse of the *Ruth Isabella* with a kind of fraught impatience. She looked as if she had not slept, and smoked cigarette after cigarette. Here in the south of Baltasay the visibility was even worse than in the town and a grey wall of cloud meant that they would not see the boat until it was almost at the jetty.

George walked up to Sylvia. More than ever now he wanted to finish the thing quickly. While he was standing at the bar, the night before, it had occurred to him that he should just fly south, leave Baltasay and Kinness, and never return. Even while he had been drunk, however, that had seemed impossible and his conversation with Johnson had made it essential that he complete the matter before he left.

"You must be glad to be going home," he said. She did not seem glad. She seemed frightened, desperately unhappy.

"Yes."

"Who telephoned you from Kinness?"

She stared at him blankly.

"What do you mean?"

"While you were staying in the hotel at Baltasay, a man with a Kinness accent telephoned you. Who would that have been?"

"You're wrong," she said. "The only phone call I had was from Jonathan."

But she twisted the wedding ring round and round on her finger.

It was a monotonous journey back to the island and George looked at his watch with increasing impatience. The sea was flat calm and the mist was so dense that there were no seabirds to watch. After Alec's outburst at the plane the day before, George had expected some comment from him, but he said nothing. Perhaps

Sandy had explained that George was carrying out the investigation with his blessing.

As they approached Kinness the cloud lifted a little and there were a few moments of sunshine. Everything at the jetty there was the same as it always was. The men performed the acts of throwing and tying ropes with their usual easy grace. James was there with the lorry. The islanders worked together to unload the boat's cargo. There were shouts of friendship, jokes, laughter. The island was green and fresh after the rain.

Jonathan had been waiting for Sylvia, and the couple walked together immediately towards the school house. George watched them carefully. He saw Sylvia smile at Jonathan but it seemed to him false and mechanical, as if she were still thinking of something else.

Sarah had been there to meet Jim. She waved at George, but she was watching her husband. She stood with the men on the lorry and helped to unload sacks of flour. He thought that he had been unfair to separate her from her new family by involving her in the investigation. He would complete the thing by himself. He saw Sarah and Jim smile at each other and thought bitterly: they don't care that an old man and a child have died. It means nothing to them. The cloud came down again and there was a light persistent rain.

When he got to the school house, Sylvia was upstairs unpacking and Jonathan was alone in the sitting room. His hair was wet and tousled and he looked very young and confused.

"I don't understand her," he said. "I don't know what she wants. You did give her my message?"

"Yes."

"What did she say?"

"She said that she thought it might be too late to make a fresh start."

"She hasn't said that much to me. She won't talk to me. She seems so unhappy. I didn't realize that she was so miserable." He looked up from the fire. "Do you think it's too late for us?"

"I don't know," George said. "How should I know?"

It was nearly dark but he went outside. He walked down the road to the post office. The door was open and the light was on inside the shop. Annie was stacking shelves from boxes and crates which had arrived on the boat. Kenneth had just arrived back from delivering the island mail and was taking off his wet jacket. There was no sign of Elspeth and the boy. The Dances did not see George. He waited outside in the wet and the dark and he listened to them.

"Where are they?" Kenneth asked. His voice was low.

"She's giving Ben his tea."

"What was the letter she had?"

"It was from her solicitor. Bain lost his appeal."

"That will be a relief to her."

"Yes. She didn't seem surprised. It was as if she had expected it." Annie paused. She was standing on some steps, stacking tins of peas on a high shelf. She had a duster in one hand and was wiping tins before putting them on the shelf. She stopped her work, came down the steps, and approached her husband. She was still clutching the duster.

"She wants to tell everyone," she said. "After managing to keep it to ourselves for so long. She says she can't stand the strain of keeping it secret anymore."

"But there's no need." His voice louder now and quite excitable. "The police said that they'd be discreet, that there was no need for anyone to know. I thought they were very decent."

"It's not that. She said that she'd decided to make it public before she spoke to the police."

She waited, expecting some response from her husband, and when none came she continued:

"She says she had to face it. It was her responsibility and she has to face it."

"I don't know what to say," Kenneth said. "I don't know what to do for the best anymore."

George stepped forward and knocked on the door. They were startled.

"I'm sorry," he said. "I didn't mean to surprise you."

"What do you want?" Kenneth Dance asked rudely.

George walked into the room. The door was still open behind him and he could hear the island noises in the darkness: the sea and the animals in the field behind the house. He shut the door and it became just another room.

"I know about Elspeth," he said. "I have to talk about it."

They stared at him. The bewildered, gaping faces should have been ludicrous, but he understood their horror and felt only pity and distaste.

"Who's been talking?" Kenneth Dance said at last.

"No one. Why? Does somebody on Kinness know about it?"

"No," Kenneth Dance shouted. "How could they?"

"I was wondering if perhaps Mary knew."

"The child? How could she have found out?"

"She was friends with Ben. He might have told her."

"No," Annie answered quietly. "You don't understand. He won't talk about it to anyone. The doctor explained that it's too painful for him to think about it. She wouldn't have found out from him."

"I see," George said. "I'm sorry. I had to ask. You do understand?"

They said nothing and he turned to go.

"Mr. Palmer-Jones!" Kenneth Dance called him back. "You won't say anything?"

Dance knew in a way that the words were an insult, but he had to be sure.

"No," George said. "That's for your daughter to do."

George took the road to Sandwick. It was quicker over the fields, but there was no moon and he was not sure enough of the way. The extra distance he had to walk frustrated him. When he reached the house the lights were on and the curtains were drawn. Agnes opened the door to him.

"I'm sorry to disturb you," George said. "I was hoping to speak to Will."

"He's in his bedroom. Shall I call him down?"

"No. That's all right. I'll go upstairs to him."

He knew that once Will came downstairs they would have no privacy. She showed him the way and he knocked at the bedroom door.

Will was surprised to see him, but welcomed him in. He was listening to a tape of an Irish folk group, but turned off the cassette recorder and moved books and files from a chair so that George could sit down. It was a typical teenager's bedroom. The remnants of childhood were still there—the board games and photographs of footballers—but there was a CND poster on the wall and Will's own sketches of plants and birds.

"Jonathan has just phoned," Will said. "To ask me to go ringing with him tonight. He wants to catch the swans on Silver Water. I thought I'd go. It would be something to do. Sarah was here when he phoned and she's asked if she can come, too."

"I want to talk to you about Elspeth," George said. "You know, don't you, why she was so upset at the sale in the hall?"

"No," Will said quickly. "I don't know." But he was blushing.

"We don't need to discuss it," George said. "I don't want to know any details. I just need to know if you told anyone else."

The boy hesitated.

"Of course not."

"You didn't tell Mary? Didn't you even hint to her that Elspeth might be hiding something she might be ashamed of?"

"Of course not. How could I? Mary was dead."

"Then you didn't see the report of the original court case last March?"

"No. I didn't know anything about it until I went out to school on Monday. I don't usually buy a paper, so I didn't read about the case in March. Someone had left a paper on my seat on the bus which collected us at Lutwick and took us to the high school. I recognized Elspeth at once. It was horrible. I hid the paper in one of my bags so that the younger children wouldn't see it."

"So you didn't know about Elspeth before Mary died; you couldn't have told her?"

"No."

George had been so sure that he had found Mary's secret at last. He had been certain that the child had learnt enough about Elspeth's past to taunt the Dance family, even if she did not realize the implications of what she said. He had been convinced that Will had seen the publicity surrounding the original court case and had passed the information to Mary. Now it was impossible. If Mary had no way of knowing that Ben had been ill treated and that Elspeth and her husband had been in court, then the theory would not work and he would have to start from the beginning again.

Will sat hunched on the bed and waited for more questions, but George left the room and almost ran down the stairs. At the bottom Sandy was waiting for him.

"George," he said. "My friend. Have you anything to tell us? The police were here again yesterday asking questions but they won't talk to me."

"No," George said. "I thought that I'd come close to it, but it won't work."

"You will find out?"

"Yes. I'll find out."

It was a relief to be outside again, away from the questions, the worried faces. It seemed that the stability of the island, preserved by the philosophy of keeping up appearances, was under threat, and that the strict code of conduct was not strong enough to prevent the tension and anger coming to the surface and exploding. It's not fair, he thought. It's not really my business. It shouldn't be my responsibility to hold the place together.

He was angry with himself because he had relied so heavily on the theory that Mary had known about Elspeth, but he could not relinquish it. Perhaps Kenneth and Annie are lying, he thought. Perhaps Ben talks about his father being in prison to anyone who will listen, but they don't want to admit it. For a moment he thought he would return to the post office, demand to see the child, ask him if he had grown close enough to Mary to confide in her. But that was clearly impossible.

Jonathan might know, he thought with a spark of hope. If Ben had mentioned his father at school or if he and Mary were especially close, then Jonathan should know.

In Unsta, on the surface at least, there was no sense that that the structure of the island was under attack. Sarah and Jim sat in complacent cosiness by the kitchen fire. There was a sports programme on the radio, but they were not listening to it. Jim was reading. He had been up early to go out with the boat. Sarah felt very healthy and well, physically content. She had been up early too, to help Maggie with the Buness milking. She missed the challenge and commitment of nursing more than she had expected, but she was, slowly, starting to make herself useful. Physical activity had become a reasonable substitute.

Sarah lay back in her chair and stretched her stockinged feet towards the fire.

"I'm not sure I want to go out tonight now," she said.

Jim grunted, turned lazily towards her, and looked up from his magazine.

"You don't need to go," he said. "Give Will a ring. He can go by himself."

"No," she said. "I promised. And it'll be interesting. Besides, I want to find out why George went to Baltasay."

He put down his magazine.

"I don't think you should meddle with that anymore," he said. "Not now that the police are involved."

"Do they really believe that Robert was murdered?"

"Yes."

"It doesn't seem possible," she said. "When George was talking about Mary being pushed over the cliff, he was very plausible and convincing, but I never took it seriously. Then Robert was shot and it all started again." She took Jim's hand. "The police did believe that you were just shooting rabbits on our land?"

"I think so. They were more interested in finding out about the old man and who had a grudge against him."

"He seemed harmless enough," she said. "I can't imagine him offending anyone."

"He was an irritating old fool, always on the scrounge, sticking his nose into other people's business. No one here liked him."

"But you can't think of anyone who would have murdered him?"

"Perhaps not. But I can't think of many who would rock the boat to find out who did."

She was quiet. She did not want to spoil their peace together with an argument, but it seemed quite wrong to her. She began to move around, finding warm clothes and waterproofs.

"Perhaps you'd better not go tonight," he said. "Palmer-Jones has been asking a lot of questions. It isn't liked. They think he's some sort of police spy. Perhaps you'd better keep your distance."

"Will is going."

"He's still a boy."

"You said that I should do what I thought was right."

She thought that he was going to persist, demand that she stay at home, but he shrugged. "You'd better go, then," he said.

She sat down again on the chair by the fire and began to lace up her boots.

"I'd better walk up to Sandwick with you," he said, trying to be friendly again. She smiled at him, grateful for his effort.

"No," she said. "Will is coming here to collect me."

"Take care, then."

"Don't worry," she said. "No one's going to shoot at me."

Chapter Thirteen

George could not understand why Jonathan was so obsessed with catching the swans. The whole thing seemed to him to be a nightmare. He had expected that Jonathan would have used the time while George was at the post office, to talk to Sylvia. He had thought that they would have had a quiet meal together, that they might have reached some understanding about leaving Kinness. But when he returned to the school house from Sandwick, Jonathan was frantically gathering rings and pliers ready for the expedition and Sylvia was nowhere to be seen.

"We'll get them," Jonathan said. "Tonight, we'll get them."

"Why the rush? Why tonight?" He had other things to discuss with Jonathan.

"There's no moon," Jonathan said, "and the birds could go at any time. Will and the Stennet girl are coming, too."

"I know. Where's Sylvia?"

"She's coming with us. She's just gone to get ready. We were waiting until you came back to eat."

"I thought you might want to be alone."

"No need for that," Jonathan said with forced heartiness. "We always like company."

You're frightened to be alone with her, George thought. You're frightened of what she might say to you. And she's trying to avoid it, too.

"I wanted to ask you about one of your pupils," George said, quickly, wanting to avoid talking in front of Sylvia. "It's Elspeth's son."

"Yes?" Jonathan was packing the ringing equipment into a small rucksack and George had only half his attention.

"What surname does he use at school?"

"Dance. I think I've got the father's name somewhere, but I can't remeber what it is. Elspeth said that she'd taken her maiden name again as soon as she'd separated and she'd prefer it used at school. I couldn't see any problem."

"Did you ever meet the father?"

"Only at the wedding. Elspeth came back occasionally on holiday but she only brought the boy."

"They were married on the island?"

"No. They had a quiet wedding in Glasgow. Then we heard that the baby had arrived not very long after."

"Has Ben ever mentioned his father in school?"

"No. I heard the other kids asking once in the playground where his dad was and what he did. He said that his dad was dead. He seems to have stuck to that story."

"Isn't he rather young to have maintained a lie like that?"

"I don't think so. He's a very bright child, very mature for his age. But perhaps Elspeth has told him that his father is dead and he believes her."

"You don't know anything about the father?"

"Nothing."

"Was Ben especially friendly with Mary Stennet?"

"I don't understand," Drysdale said. "You can't think that Ben had anything to do with the child's death."

"I don't know." George was too impatient to hide his exasperation. "Please. Just accept that I need the information."

"Mary was the oldest child in the school. Occasionally she overwhelmed the little ones. She latched on to Ben. The others had been smothered by her for too long and were glad that she'd found another victim. He seemed not to mind her attentions but they certainly weren't friends. There was a great difference in their ages but he was the more grown up. He tolerated her but he wasn't dependent on her."

"Her death doesn't seem to have upset him?"

"No."

That was it. He could persist with his precious theory no longer. If Mary had not learnt of Elspeth's secret from Will or Ben, then she could not have known about it. At the back of his mind there was another idea, an explanation for Mary's death and Robert's, an explanation which fitted all the facts, but before he could explore it properly Sylvia came in. She was dressed in jeans and a heavy jersey, but she was wearing a lot of make-up. The moody preoccupation had gone and she seemed possessed by a disturbing and feverish gaiety. What fun it would be, she said, to catch the swans. How beautiful they would be in the torchlight. She longed to stroke them. She ran her finger along her husband's forehead, pushing the hair away from his eyes. He was her swan, she said.

George found the scene shocking and embarrassing.

"Why don't we put it off for another night?" he demanded. "Why is everyone so desperate to catch the swans?"

"It's a lovely night," Sylvia said. "Look outside. It's a lovely night."

"It's raining," George said.

But it made no difference. They were determined to ring the swans. It seemed to George that the evening proceeded with an awful inevitability, and at such a pace that he had no time to reconsider the facts surrounding his investigation, no time to think clearly at all.

They ate a hurried meal surrounded by the debris needed to ring the swans. Both Jonathan and Sylvia talked continuously, though there was little communication. Jonathan talked about his plans for the evening. Sylvia relived her stay on Baltasay, described the things she had bought, the places she had visited. Despite the flying words he found that his new idea was growing stronger. He longed for quiet, a time to himself. He regretted the time wasted in his rush around the island from the post office to Sandwick, the wasted words.

"I don't think I'll come," he said, suddenly. "I don't feel very well. I'll stay here."

"Nonsense," said Jonathan. "Whooper swan must be a ringing tick. You'll never have the opportunity again."

It was true and he was beginning to feel that he should be there with them out on the hill and that in their present excitable state they needed protecting from their own folly.

Will and Sarah arrived soon after they had finished eating. Sylvia greeted them effusively. Jonathan drew them immediately into plans for the evening. Will was wearing a long army-surplus overcoat, very similar to one George's son had possessed at a similar age. The reminder of his family made George feel isolated, like a traveller in a foreign land who has just received a letter from home. He no longer wanted to involve Sarah in his investigation and he answered her whispered inquiry about his trip to Baltasay politely but noncommittally. Throughout the evening Will maintained a cool adolescent aloofness, as if the adults' antics were beyond his comprehension and he participated only through boredom. Sarah, however, seemed to catch the Drysdales' mood and became as lively and frivolous as they were.

They went outside into the rain and climbed into Jonathan's Old Land Rover. George sat next to Jonathan and heard Sarah and Sylvia laughing in the back. It seemed to him that Jonathan drove recklessly, but the others seemed to enjoy the speed. The conditions, George had to admit, were perfect. There was no wind, and as they drove past Kell the cloud was so low that they could hardly see the lighted square of the kitchen window. Then the road turned into a track and the laughter in the back was louder as the Land Rover bounced and jolted over ruts and boulders.

"Have you ever done any dazzling?" Jonathan shouted above the noise of the engine and the women's screams.

"Only waders."

"It's the same principle. If you shine a very bright light at a bird, it seems to daze it. Then someone gets behind the swan and catches it. It won't be easy, but sometimes they actually walk towards the light. They seem stunned by it."

The track ended in front of the lighthouse. Not many years before, three families had lived there. The light-keepers' cottages were still there, the windows boarded up. Everything had been left—washing lines, a children's swing in one of the gardens, a rusting wheelbarrow. It was as if the people had all left quite suddenly and mysteriously. George was reminded of other islands where the whole population had been evacuated because so few people remained. In his torchlight the lighthouse compound evoked the same sad and empty feeling. The beam of the light swung above them, regular, remote, and impersonal. It was switched on automatically now as the daylight faded. Each time it swung above their heads it illuminated the cliffs of a nearby headland. George remembered Mary and thought that it had been right to send the men and their families away. It was not a safe place for children.

The others were unloading the Land Rover with whispered giggles. Jonathan was worried that they would frighten away the swans and was trying to keep them quiet.

He and Will had thigh waders, so they would go into the water to catch the swans.

"I want to hold the torch," Sylvia said. "I want to work the magic on them."

"You won't hold it steady. Let George to it."

"No," she said, sulky as a child. "I want to do it." And she was given her own way.

The pool they called Silver Water was away from the road, over moorland too boggy to take the Land Rover safely, in a dip in the hills, quite close to the edge of the cliff. To George it hardly seemed bigger than a village duckpond.

Jonathan made them switch off their torches before they started, and they stumbled and splashed through the peat bog. Sylvia and Sarah went arm in arm, giggling together, but Jonathan was taking it very seriously. They stopped just as the land rose and became drier. Jonathan wriggled forward on his stomach and peered over the rocky mound and down to the pool. The swans were there, he whispered. He could hear them. Sylvia would go down to the water one way, with the torch, and he and Will would go the other. George hoped that he would be left alone then. He had known why Robert had been killed right from the beginning. Now he knew why Mary had been murdered and the identity of the murderer could only be one of three people. If he had time, he had the facts to work the thing out. Tomorrow, he thought, it will all be over. But Jonathan would not let him sit alone. He sent George down the bank with Sylvia, saying that he did not trust her to dazzle the birds properly.

So George slithered down the bank after Sylvia. She was crouched by the water, holding the torch with both hands, concentrated and intense. He did not know what had happened to Sarah. They waited to give Jonathan and Will a chance to get into position, then George touched her arm and she switched on the torch. It had a new battery and the light was fierce. The swans were much closer than he had expected. Because he and Sylvia were crouched so low to the water, the birds seemed enormous. They were huge white monsters. There were only three of them and they seemed transfixed, held by the charm of the powerful light. Beyond the birds George could see Jonathan and Will approaching, arms outstretched, ready to jump. They'll only get one each, George thought. They'll have to let the other one go. He could hear the water slapping against their waders.

Then there was a gunshot. It seemed to come from behind him and it seemed very close. Somebody screamed and Sylvia must have dropped the torch because suddenly there was no light but the arc of the lighthouse beam swinging relentlessly far above them. The swans honked and the noise seemed louder than the gunshot. He could feel the air from their wing beats as they prepared to fly. There was another gunshot and a thud and a splash. They've killed one of the swans, George thought with a rising anger. He stood and turned to face the murderer. The circling spotlight clipped the top of the rocky hillock above him and he thought he saw a silhouette, but it moved on before he could be sure. George began to climb the bank, furious because the swan was dead, and he heard the two remaining whoopers fly above him. At the top of the bank George stopped. He could see and hear nothing. Sylvia must have dropped the torch into the water because it had not been switched on again. The beam from the lighthouse approached, then blinded him. He heard the sound of footsteps on the concrete path which led from the empty cottages to the lighthouse, then a door banged. Whoever had fired the shots was taking refuge in the lighthouse. He ran on. The cold water of the bog trickled inside his Wellingtons and splashed his trousers. He swore because he was so old and moved so slowly. His breath came in gulping gasps.

Afterwards he admitted that it was ridiculous to go into the lighthouse alone. He should have waited for the others. Once inside, there was no escape for the murderer. But in his mind he held the image of the swan preparing to fly, upright, head to the sky, wings beating, and then the shot in the chest. He was angry and the anger clouded his judgement. And stronger than anger was curiosity. He believed that he knew who was hiding in the lighthouse, but he wanted to be certain. The impatience to complete the investigation, which had been growing all day, reached a climax. He wanted that certainty now.

The door at the bottom of the tower had been padlocked. The padlock was open, hooked into a metal ring on the door frame, and the door banged against it. He wished he had a torch, but there must have been some emergency lighting in the room at the top, because a dim light fell down the spiral stone steps. George was not frightened. He had a confidence, an arrogance, that the murderer at the top of the steps would want to speak to him. If they could sit together and talk without interruption, George was certain that he would convince the person to give him the shotgun and go with him peacefully.

George shouted up the tower. He tried to keep his voice calm and friendly, but the echo of the stone tower distorted it. There was no reply.

"I'm coming up," George called. He really thought he had nothing to fear, but he did feel tense, excited. He remembered playing hide and seek as a boy in the gloomy house where he had lived with his father, and there was the same racing heart, the same exhilaration. He no longer felt old, although the steps were steep and the tower was high. The light was stronger and the shadows on the steps were more dramatic, but George did not hesitate.

"I'm coming in now," he said. "There's no need to be afraid."

There was a door into the room where the lightkeepers must have stayed when they were on watch. It was slightly open.

"I'm coming in now," he repeated.

He pushed the door wider with one hand, but he did not go in. In the round room there was nothing. No furniture and no murderer. A short flight of metal stairs led to a balcony where the lenses and enormous stack of batteries were. He could not see the complete circle of the balcony, just a small segment through the open door.

"Why don't you come down?" he said quietly. "I won't hurt you."

He stepped into the room. There was the rustle of clothes behind him. Hiding behind the door, George thought, but he had no time to move. As he lost consciousness there was a feeling of astonishment that he could have been so foolish.

When he woke he knew that he had only been unconscious for a short time. He knew where he was at once. Sarah was bending over him.

"What are you doing here?" he asked.

"I followed you. I thought you must have come in here."

"Did you see who it was?"

"No. They must have run away just before I got here."

"What are the others doing?"

"They say that they're looking for whoever fired the shots, but they're making so much noise that they've no chance."

"I think," George said, "that I must have been hit by the gun." He raised himself on to one elbow and felt sick.

"You'd better help me up," he said. "I have things to do."

"Not tonight." She was quite firm. She could have been in a hospital ward.

"I'm a nurse, don't forget. And ..." She hesitated.

"And I'm an old man," he said.

It was exactly what she had been going to say, and she laughed.

"All the same," she said. "You must rest tonight, or you'll have headaches and dizziness for months."

"When the old nurse retires here," he said, "you could take her place."

"I could, couldn't I?" It was like a promise, a future she could look forward to and enjoy, a way of not losing touch with her past. She felt grateful to him.

"Do you know who it was?" she asked.

"Yes."

"Who was it?"

He sat up carefully.

"I thought," he said, "that I was supposed to rest."

By the time he had walked with Sarah's help down the steps and was outside, Jonathan, Sylvia, and Will were waiting by the Land Rover.

"It's no good," Jonathan said. "They'll be halfway down the island by now."

Then they saw that George was hurt. Sylvia took no part in the general demand for explanation of his injury, the concern.

"Who was it?" she asked, interrupting the others. "Did you see who it was?"

George ignored her question and allowed himself to be lifted into the Land Rover. There he swore them all to secrecy. No one on the island must know about the gunshots. He wanted no panic, no one making wild guesses, taking the law into their own hands. Despite the stabbing headache and waves of nausea, he felt in control.

"Please," he said, "don't tell anyone. It won't be much longer now. Tomorrow it will all be over. I'd finish it tonight but Sarah won't let me."

They took him back to the school house. He asked Jonathan to help him to bed.

"Don't let Sylvia go out tonight," he said when they were alone. "Keep her with you."

"Why should she want to go out now? What is it all about?"

"Tomorrow," George said. "You'll know tomorrow," and he sent Jonathan away before he undressed.

Now he was quite sure what had happened, and he slept.

Chapter Fourteen

It was Sunday. The death of an old man and the interference of the police would make no difference to the domestic Sunday ritual. The older women would have prepared all the food a day before. The tradition was beginning to change and Maggie would cook a traditional roast lunch for the whole family after church, but no one would dare to hang washing on a line or be seen working in a garden. They would all go to church in the morning, have a family midday meal, then in the afternoon if the sun was shining they would walk up the island, solemnly, like Edwardians taking the air at a seaside promenade. The children would be allowed to run on the beach and wear themselves out so that they would sit quietly through the evening service at the church. There was no television on a Sunday.

At Kell Melissa milked the cow, while James sat in white starched shirt sleeves at the kitchen table and put the finishing touches to his sermon. They were a critical congregation on Kinness, and genuinely devout. They would discuss his sermon at their lunch tables and if they disagreed with the sentiments expressed in it he would get to hear of it.

He was happy to let Melissa milk the cow. She had been up before him, and when he came downstairs he noticed that her waterproofs were wet from the drizzle which had persisted all night. There was a pan of porridge ready on the stove. He did not want to look too closely for an explanation for the dramatic change in her. She was content and that was the most important thing. He tried to clear his mind of anything else.

Ben had woken, early in the morning, with nightmares. Elspeth heard him screaming and screaming, and rushed to comfort him. She tried to take him in her arms but he pushed her away, even after he had woken. She thought that he was quiet and had gone back to her own bed but he had begun screaming again and this time had raised the whole household. He had slept at last in Annie's and Kenneth's bed.

Because of the disturbed night they were late waking and it was a rush to have breakfast and to dress for church. There was no question that they would miss the morning service. That would have been unthinkable. Yet rather than looking forward to the worship as a time of peace, they were dreading it.

"I'm going to tell everyone," Elspeth had said. "After church."

"No," said Kenneth, horrified. "You don't know what it will mean to us. You must consider again."

"I'm going for a walk," she said. "Don't follow me. I won't do anything foolish. I will think about it and see you in church."

Ben watched the conversation, red-eyed and tired behind a bowl of cornflakes, as if he did not know what they were talking about. Will hated the mornings. In the hostel he always missed breakfast. He made instant coffee in his room and arrived at school at half past nine after assembly had finished. It was breaking the rules but allowance was made for sixth formers.

Agnes tried to get him out of bed to have breakfast with the rest of the family. His disgust at being woken from a deep sleep gave him the words which he had been struggling to find since he had returned home. He spoke without thinking. She should leave him alone, he said. He did not want to be there anyway. He had only come back because she had been so insistent and he was going back to school as soon as there was an available plane. Then he turned over and went back to sleep. Agnes stood in the kitchen and wept. She had lost Mary and Will. Nothing would be the same again.

In Buness the boys were in their room changing into their

Sunday-best clothes. Maggie was washing the breakfast dishes and Alec was polishing his shoes.

"You should have done that last night," she said.

"I know." He was irritated. "I forgot."

"So Sylvia Drysdale came back on the boat yesterday," she said, working on the petty irritation he already felt, trying to provoke a reaction.

"Look," he said. "I've told you. There never was anything to that. It was just gossip."

"No," she said. "You never did tell me."

"Well I'm telling you now. There was never anything in it."

"I'm glad," she said, "that you've told me." But it did not help her and she felt uneasy and tense.

Sarah took it for granted that they were going to church, but Jim refused.

"No," he said, "we agreed. We decided to go last week because Mother was so upset, but that was all. We wouldn't go again."

He was adamant.

"You can go," he said, "but I won't think a lot of you if you do. It'll only be for appearances."

She was surprised because he took it so seriously.

"Did you enjoy yourself last night?" he asked, to change the subject.

"Oh," she said vaguely, "I'll tell you all about it later. Do you think that Alec would lend me his car?"

George woke early. He got out of bed and opened the curtains. The cloud was still low over the hill. There would be no chance of the police coming in by plane. There was no movement in the house. He dressed and went downstairs, then left the house quietly. It was just as well, he thought, not to have an audience.

As he went through the gate on to the road a car pulled up and stopped. It was Sarah in Alec's car.

"You shouldn't be walking," she said. "I thought you could do with a lift."

"Nonsense. Fresh air and exercise is good for concussion. You're afraid of missing something."

"It's not that," she said. "I didn't want anything else to happen to you. At the beginning I thought you were just a crank, and that Mary's death was an accident. Then Robert died and the police were here with their questions and you seemed to know so much more than them. Then when I found you last night, I thought you were dead, too. It was horrible."

Has it come to this? he thought. A girl younger than my daughter thinks that she can protect me! But he said nothing. He got into the car and told her where to go.

"Do you want me to stay in the car?" she asked when they arrived.

"Would you prefer that?"

"No."

"Come on in then. It might be useful to have a witness."

He was glad that she was there.

They sat in the kitchen at Kell, much as they had done on their previous visit. Melissa had changed into her best dress for church, but she made tea for them. James watched her with anxious, protective eyes. He had put on the jacket of his suit, and when they came in he looked at his watch. He did not want to be late for the service.

George slowly took the green silk scarf from his pocket and laid it on the table. He touched it carefully, laid it out so that they would see the pattern and the colours. James' eyes seemed drawn to it, but he looked at his watch again.

"Last time I came," George said, "I asked you about this scarf. You had no opportunity to answer then. I'll ask you again. Did you see it after Mary died?"

He spoke to James. There was silence. The window was open and they could hear the hens in the yard outside. They were looking at James and it came as a shock when Melissa spoke.

"You'll have to tell them, James."

He looked at her, unsure, upset. He looked very distinguished,

Sarah thought. A small, trim man with grey hair and a dark suit. He could have been a judge or a retired admiral.

"I don't want any more lies," Melissa said. She seemed relieved to be speaking, completely relaxed. "He found it in my things. He never talked about it, but he took it away. I thought perhaps he'd burnt it. Then you brought it back here. I thought you must know what had happened. I was afraid even that James had taken the scarf to you and told you where he found it, but I should have known better than that. Since then I've been waiting for you to come again. I'm glad that it's over."

"I don't understand . . ." Sarah supposed that she should leave it all to George, but she was too involved to remain silent.

"Why I did it? I regretted it, you know, the moment it was done. I have been a little mad for a long time now. It was so unfair that Agnes should have had so many children while I had none. Mary should have been my child. I would have cared for her properly. She wouldn't have been a wild, unkind girl if she had been my daughter."

"You wrote the note pinned to my wedding dress," Sarah said. "You thought that Jim should have belonged to you, too."

Melissa seemed angry that she had been interrupted. It was as if she had prepared her speech and Sarah had spoiled he performance. But she answered.

"I wrote the note. They brought the dress up here for me to iron it. They know that I'm good with my hands. It wasn't a tactful thing to have done. I have no children to dress up on their wedding day. And she should never have named the lad after my husband. I would have used that name if I'd had a son."

"But you never went out that night," Sarah said. "You were at home all evening."

"I went to watch. I wanted to see what you looked like. I wanted to see what was going on. If my son was being married, I should have been there."

"What happened?" Again it was Sarah who asked the question. George Palmer-Jones watched the conversation between the women in silence. It was impossible to guess what he was thinking.

"Mary was running around the hall in some sort of game. The music was still playing. I was about to go home. There was nothing more to see and I knew that soon it would be the interval and the people would come out."

"She must have been hiding from Maggie," Sarah said. "She was supposed to be helping her."

"She must have heard my footsteps on the road because she saw me. She called me a witch, a spying old witch. Children can be cruel to people they don't belong to. She came at me, calling names. I didn't want to face her, so I ran off up the hill?"

"Up Ellie's Head?"

"Yes. But she chased after me, calling names all the time. She followed me right to the edge and I pushed her. I thought; now Agnes knows what it is like to lose a child."

"And Robert? Why did you kill him?" Sarah spoke again, because she wanted to know and because George was remaining resolutely, infuriatingly silent.

"He saw me outside the hall that night and later he guessed. He came to see me."

At the beginning James had looked bewildered, but confusion was turning to horror. Tears were rolling down his face. He stood up.

"No!" he shouted at her. "No." He simply wanted to stop her talking, as if silence would erase the meaning of what she had said.

"Sit down, James," she said calmly. "It's the only way."

"So Mary never had a secret," Sarah said. "We were wrong all the time."

James seemed not to hear her.

"No," he said. "It's not the only way."

"Mary did have a secret," George said, very quietly, "didn't she, Melissa?"

As George turned his attention from James to Melissa, James got up and walked out of the room. It's been too much for him, Sarah thought. He's lived with this woman for more than thirty years. He believed that he knew her and now he's found out that she killed two people. He can't face it. She thought, even, that he might be physically sick. He looked very ill. When George got up and almost ran after James, she thought he was being insensitive. The man obviously wanted to be on his own.

"Don't be a fool, man," Melissa screamed after her husband. "I've told you. It's the only way."

James was a little younger than George and much fitter. He still worked the croft. I've spent too long sitting behind a desk, George thought. I won't catch him.

James knew exactly where he was going. He ran round the back of the house, past the sheep pen, and through a field of oats. He had still not buttoned the black jacket of his suit and it flapped at the sides as he ran. He looks like a hooded crow with a sleek grey head and black wings, George thought as he walked through the wet stalks of the oats. He went as fast as he could, hoping James might wait for him, that he might after all want to talk.

After the fields of the croft the land sloped down to the sea. George watched James run to the edge of the cliff, to Kell Geo where all the rubbish from the island was dumped, because the water was so deep—all the tin cans, and the rusty cars that would go no more. He watched James pause for a second at the top, then saw him fling himself over to land with the garbage underneath the sea.

George walked slowly to the cliff edge. As soon as James left Kell, George knew that it would end like this. He had been incompetent. He should have foreseen it, but since his arrival at Kell nothing had gone as he had planned. He heard a movement behind him and turned round. He had expected to see Sarah, but it was Elspeth:

"You saw James?" he said.

"Yes. He meant to do it, didn't he? He did it on purpose?"

"Yes."

"Why would he do that?"

"He killed an old man. And a child."

When he returned to Kell, the two women were still sitting, staring at each other across the kitchen table. It was as if they were waiting for him before resuming their conversation. Sarah heard George coming and looked up with relief. Her psychiatric training had only been for six weeks. It had not equipped her to deal with murderers. But George ignored her.

"I'm sorry," he said to Melissa. "He was too fast for me."

"He's dead," she said. It was a statement, not a question, and it did not need an answer.

"Would you leave us alone, Sarah?" he said.

She got up.

"I'll leave you the car," she said. "I'll walk." Then: "I don't know what to tell them all."

"Tell them nothing."

She walked down the island. The church bell was ringing for the morning service. She imagined the congregation sitting, waiting for James to stand before them to offer the usual words of the Christian peace and reassurance.

"He won't come!" she shouted to the sheep. She lurched out of the mist on to the road. "He's dead."

She went home to Unsta, and she saw no one.

Chapter Fifteen

It was evening before George was ready to speak to them to explain it all. He was with Melissa all morning. He hardly spoke, but he listened intently to what she was saying. When James did not arrive at church, Sandy telephoned Kell to find out where he was. Melissa and George were so engrossed in their conversation that they let the telephone ring. Kenneth Dance took the service.

Then George went to the school house. He phoned the nurse from there and asked her to go to Kell to be with Melissa. He talked to Sylvia and Jonathan. First he spoke to Sylvia alone. It was the most difficult interview of his career. Afterwards he went out and walked in the playground, pacing backwards and forwards.

I knew who it was, he thought. I was right about that. But I botched it at the end.

When he went back in, the Drysdales had decided to leave, as soon as the mist had cleared for a plane to come to collect them. Sylvia was starting to pack.

He told Sandy that he would go to Sandwick to explain it and he had expected all the Stennets to be there, but it was only Sandy and Agnes, Sarah and Jim. Will, too, was packing, hoping to get a plane back to school the next day, and Alec and Maggie had not been invited.

It was not dark outside, but the electric light was on in the sitting room and the heavy curtains were drawn. There was an enormous fire in the grate and the room was very hot. Agnes sat in a rocking chair near to the fire and was knitting. She would never usually have picked up her knitting on a Sunday, but she needed the comfort of it and thought that the Lord would understand. Sarah sat on the floor beside her. Jim let George into the house and Sandy rushed out of the sitting room to greet him. When they had all sat down, he said:

"George, who killed our daughter?"

"It was James."

Agnes looked up, but continued to knit ferociously.

"Tell us about it," she said. "Why did he do it?"

"Because she knew his secret and he was afraid that she would tell."

"What was his secret?" Jim asked. "Do you know?"

"He and Sylvia Drysdale were lovers."

"No," Agnes said sharply. "He was a religious man."

"He was a frustrated man," Jim said. "You must have seen Melissa and James together, Mother. Even when she still came down the island with him to the dances, she would never let him touch her."

"He would never have gone with a woman like Sylvia Drysdale."

"She is very attractive," George said, "and she did care for him. It's been going on for a long time. I think he tried to stop it, more than once, but they had become dependent on each other. He needed the physical contact and she liked to feel that she was wanted. Melissa guessed, I think, what was happening. She was perhaps even a little relieved."

"They must have been very careful," Sarah said. "It can't be easy to keep a secret on Kinness."

"It started when Melissa sent James to ask Sylvia to visit her," George said, "but Sylvia and James very rarely met in the school house after that. James still had a key to the lighthouse. He was paid to do maintenance work up there, and that's where they met. Probably in one of the cottages. Mary must have seen them on one of the few occasions when he went to the school house. She used to wander into Sylvia's room and try on her jewellery and make-up. Perhaps it was a time when they thought they were safe, during school hours. Perhaps Mary wandered up in one of her breaks and saw them together. I think that's what must have happened. They didn't even know she'd seen them. Mary didn't say anything to Sylvia, but she began to drop hints to James. He realized that she must know. He couldn't face the shame of the affair being public knowledge. He had spent his life on Kinness telling people how to behave. It was unthinkable for his secret to come out. So he arranged to meet Mary in the interval of the dance on Ellie's Head. It had to be then because he was playing in the band. Perhaps he bribed her with a present, or more information. She waited for him by the cliff. She was deaf, so she wouldn't have heard him coming. It would have been very easy. As I found out today, he was fit. It was quite possible for him to run back to the hall to start the music for the second half of the party.

"He would probably have got away with it, if he hadn't gone back for the scarf."

"Why did he do that?" Jim asked.

"It was Sylvia's scarf. I think he went back later, when he was supposed to be searching for Mary on the hill. He knew that the relationship with Sylvia was over, and he had to have something of hers. He had a desperate passion for her. He didn't think that anyone would notice that the scarf was gone. He put it in his pocket."

George turned to Sarah.

"Do you remember when we went to talk to James and Melissa after Robert died: Melissa was quite calm until I showed her the scarf, then the panic attack started? She had seen it in James' pocket, I think, without realizing the implication of it."

"Yes," Sarah said, "I remember."

"When I first started asking questions about Mary's death, Sylvia didn't take me seriously. She didn't know, you see, that Mary had discovered her secret. She thought that the child had slipped accidentally and that I was playing detective through boredom. Perhaps I was."

"Then why did she decide to leave the island suddenly, when the *Ruth Isabella* took the children out to school?"

"Because I was asking about secrets. As I've said, she cared for James. She was afraid that I might have found out about them. It wouldn't have mattered too much for her—she had a dreadful reputation anyway—but she knew that it would have ruined him. So she decided to get out to Baltasay where she'd be well away from any questions. I must stress that she had no idea at that time that James had murdered Mary.

"On her way out to the boat James met her in the deserted croft by the road. Perhaps he had decided that he could not do without her, and he begged her to stay. Certainly he was so upset that when he left the croft he did not notice that he had dropped the silk scarf. When he went back for it later, it had gone. Ben Dance had gone to play in there before school and had found it."

"Why did he kill Robert?" Sandy, said. "He was an old fool, but he was not a threat to James."

"Robert was up on the hill the morning that James and Sylvia met in Taft. It must have been clear that there was an attachment between them. As I say, I think that James was devastated to learn that Sylvia was planning to leave the island. When she got to Baltasay, he phoned her at the hotel, probably to ask her to come back to Kinness. Perhaps they kissed, and Robert saw them. Perhaps he actually heard what they said to each other.

"Robert probably thought that he would be able to use the information—not just to make mischief like Mary—but for some sort of gain. I don't suppose he connected the relationship between Sylvia and James with Mary's death, so he didn't realize how dangerous it was to blackmail James."

"He will have asked for a goose," Sandy said suddenly. "He was always thinking of his stomach, the greedy old man, and we were all too mean to give him one."

"Whatever it was, he went that afternoon after you'd all been out shooting the geese. Perhaps he saw James down on the Loons. James would still have had his shotgun with him. It was too easy. James didn't have time to think.

"When I went to Baltasay, I told Sylvia that Robert had been murdered and that he had been on the hill above her when she had been meeting at Taft. Then she realized, I think, that James must have been the murderer."

"Why didn't she say anything to you?" Sarah asked.

"I'm sure that she would have done eventually, when she was less confused. But she loved him. She would have seen it as a betrayal."

"Love!" Agnes snapped. "She doesn't know the meaning of the word."

George answered gently. "She did love him, you know. All the secrecy was on his behalf, not her own. She only flirted with Alec so that you wouldn't think of looking elsewhere for someone to associate her with. She knew what a reputation she has."

"It was James who shot at you, when we were out ringing the swans," Sarah said.

"Yes. It was a foolish thing to do. I think by that time he was insane with fear and worry. He must have heard that I'd gone out to Baltasay on the plane. Perhaps he thought that I'd given up the investigation and gone home. Then I turned up on the *Ruth Isabella*. With Sylvia. I don't know who he was trying to hit then, up on the hill—Sylvia or me. Perhaps he was trying to frighten her into keeping quiet about their relationship or perhaps he was trying to frighten me away altogether. By that time I don't think he knew what he was doing. I don't think that he can have meant to kill either of us. He could have done that easily enough if he'd tried. After all, when I wandered into the lighthouse, I had a gentle tap on the head, not a bellyful of shot."

"You knew who it was at that time?" asked Sarah.

"Yes, though I had only worked it out that evening, as we were getting ready to ring the swans. Before that I thought that Mary's secret was quite different."

"Something to do with Elspeth?"

"Yes. But it turned out to be quite irrelevant. So I went back to the scarf. Whoever had been talking to Sylvia had dropped the scarf. From her attitude it was most likely to be a man, a lover. There weren't that many candidates. If it had been Alec, he would have been rather proud to let the island know what was going on. It had to be someone of sufficient standing for it to matter desperately if the secret came out. That meant Sandy, Kenneth Dance, or James. Then I remembered Melissa's extreme reaction when I showed her the scarf at Kell, and James' attitude to Sylvia—he emphasized over and over again how much he disapproved of her—and the thing became clear. I was certain when I realized that whoever was in the lighthouse had a key to the padlock on the door. I knew he'd been the assistant keeper there. The Northern Lights Board were most likely to choose him as a caretaker.

"I really thought that it was Melissa," Sarah said. "All day I've been thinking that it was her and that James killed himself through shame or a second-hand guilt." She looked around the room. "She was so convincing," she said, almost apologetically. "I believed every word she said."

"James couldn't let her take the blame," George said. "I'm sure that she would have gone through with it if he'd let her. She'd worked out her story to the last detail. She told me that she was an actress once, when she was young, before she came to Baltasay. Perhaps that's why her story was so plausible."

"But why did she want to protect him?" Sarah asked. "After all he'd done. He'd been unfaithful to her."

"She felt responsible. She told me that she'd never been able to do anything for James. It was her opportunity to repay him. She was proud to do it."

"Did she go out to the hall that night, as she said?"

"Yes, but only to watch you walk up from Unsta. She never saw Mary." He chose his words carefully. "Most of what she said was true. She was jealous of Agnes, desperate for a child, a little mad. She did write the note and pin it to your dress. If they'd lived somewhere different, it might have been easier. James had so much to live up to here. People expected too much from him."

It was an accusation. They sat in silence, considering what he had said. The fire had burned down and Sandy got up to put on more coal.

"We can't change too quickly here," he said. "We've too much to lose."

"But it's not a museum," Sarah said, taking Jim's hand. The words had never seemed more relevant.

"James wouldn't have had it any different here," Sandy said, stubborn, his face red in the flames. "He believed in it, too.

"But it killed your daughter."

"No," Sandy said fiercely, getting to his feet. "James killed my daughter, James, my brother. Not Melissa or the church. He knew that he'd done an evil thing and he did what he could to put it right. He had to pay."

He walked from the room. Agnes pulled the knitting needle from the belt round her waist, laid the knitting on her lap.

"He's upset," she said. "It was his brother. They were too close for him to be generous. You're young. Kinness will be yours and you'll live here in whichever way you choose."

She got to her feet, like an old lady, carefully folded her knitting, and put it in a bag, then followed her husband.

Sarah and Jim turned to George for advice, for support in their desire for change, but he deserted them, too. He let himself out of the house and they were left in the stuffy, brightly lit room. As he walked through the yard he watched Sarah draw the curtains and throw open a window.

George left the next day with the Drysdales and Will Stennet. The cloud had gone and the sun was shining. It was mild, like a spring day.

Until a new teacher could be found, Maggie Stennet took over the school. She found it harder work than she had expected, and when the new teacher came there was no criticism about the standard of lessons.

The island came to know about Elspeth and why she had left Glasgow so suddenly. Kenneth Dance made no difficulty about her explaining her past. A Stennet had murdered two people. Watching a child being battered was a minor crime in comparison. So the Dances and Stennets continued to lead their separate lives and neither family felt that it had a superior moral status to the other.

Another Dance, a distant relative, moved into Robert's old croft, Tain, and two years later he and Elspeth were married, and had children of their own. After watching James jump to his death at

Kell Geo, Elspeth seemed stronger, more decisive. She and Sarah became friends in a quiet, unemotional way.

Melissa stayed on at Kell. They had all expected her to leave Kinness, but she decided that she had nowhere else to go. There was pressure for her to leave the croft. Sandy offered to build her a bungalow at the south of the island. It was not right, it was said, for a woman to have land which could be worked by a man, which might support a family. Agnes thought that Will should have Kell. But Sarah fought on Melissa's behalf, and when Melissa grew too old and frail to do much on the croft, Jim did it all for her. She never mixed much with people on the island, but Sarah felt that it was because she chose not to, and not because she was frightened. She died at Kell, quite suddenly, when she was nearly seventy.

Even then Will did not come back. He had gone to university in Edinburgh, and when he had taken his degree he stayed on to do post-graduate work. He loved Edinburgh. When he got drunk, he talked with affection of Kinness to his pretty young girlfriends, but he only went home occasionally for holidays. He remained at the university as a lecturer.

In the spring after she had moved on to Kinness Sarah became pregnant. Jim built on to the back of Unsta a bathroom and more bedrooms. Sarah filled the house with pretty things. Jim and Alec worked their land together in a flexible partnership. They worked well together. They had the same ideas. They became quite prosperous. Sarah had twin daughters, and later she had a son. When the children had started school, the nurse retired, at last, and Sarah took over the job. Jim was still serious, still unsure whether he should admire or disapprove of her frivolous ways, but they were happy.

So everything continued on Kinness as Sandy predicted it would. Just two weeks after James had died they had a Halloween party for the children in the school, because there always was a party at Halloween. At Christmas there was carol singing and at new year there was guising. In the spring the lambs came and then it was time for ploughing and sowing. The whole island turned out for the harvest. As the years passed the story of the murders and

James' suicide became a story like the Great Storm, told and retold until it lost its power to shock. At first Jim and Sarah refused to go to church, but when the children were old enough they demanded to go to Sunday school like their friends, and it was hard then to stay away. They called their son James.

Sarah wrote to George Palmer-Jones several times after he left the island and he always replied. He was pleased, he said, to hear the Kinness news. But he never accepted her invitation to come and stay with them at Unsta. He was busy, with his new business to run.